John Long's
CAMPFIRE HOWLERS

STORIES TO AMUSE AND ENTERTAIN

ICS Books, Inc.
Merrillville, Indiana

Dedication

To Charles Tenshen Flatcher, Sensai, and James Finley. In appreciation.

Editor's Note

The provenance of jokes, limericks, doggerel, puns and wisecracks is notoriously difficult and often quite impossible to establish with any degree of confidence, much less accuracy. I have credited the originator of such material whenever possible. Therefore, I hereby offer an omnibus thanks and acknowledgment of the authors used in this book.

The author wishes to acknowledge the following for their kind permission to reprint excerpts from their published materials in this book:

ANTI-SEMITISM and RABBI ROSENBLOOM from Leo Rosten's GIANT BOOK OF LAUGHTER by Leo Rosten. Copyright © 1985 by Leo Rosten. All rights reserved. Reprinted by permission of Crown Publishers, Inc. Reprinted by permission of the William Morris Agency,Inc. on behalf of the Author Copyright © 1985 by Leo Rosten

CLOUDLAND REVISITED and THE ROAD TO MILTOWN by S.J. Perelman, copyright © 1952 and 1953 by S.J. Perelman. All rights reserved. Reprinted by permission of Harold Ober Associates Inc. First published in *The New Yorker*.

THE DIRTY NINCOMPOOP WHO EDITS THAT JOURNAL reprinted from The Arizona *Miner* and The Arizona *Sentinel*.

LECTURES ON ASTRONOMY by John Phoenix, TUSHMAKER'S TOOTHPULLERBY by John Phoneix and THE FIRST PIANO IN A MINING CAMP by Sam Davis reprinted from Mark Twain's Library of Humor.

THE LATEST IMPROVEMENTS IN ARTILLERY, JUD BROWNIN HEARS RUBY PLAY and SOMEBODY IN MY BED from NATIVE AMERICAN HUMOR by James Aswell. Copyright 1947 by Harper & Brothers. Copyright Renewed. Reprinted by permission of Harper Collins Publishers Inc.

THIRD WORLD DRIVING from HOLIDAYS IN HELL by P.J. O'Rourke. Copyright © 1988 by P.J. O'Rourke. Used by permission of Grove/Atlantic, Inc.

NO TIME FOR SERGEANTS by Mac Hyman reprinted by permission of Curtis Brown, Ltd. Copyright © 1954 by Mac Hyman.

YOU DRIVE, DEAR by Fred S. Tobey. © 1961 by H.S.D. Publications, Inc. Reprinted by permission of the author.

KINDLY DIG YOUR GRAVE by Stanley Ellin reprinted by permission of Curtis Brown, Ltd. Copyright © 1970 by Stanley Ellin.

GAMBLING by Ron Fawcett. From Leo Rosten's GIANT BOOK OF LAUGHTER by Leo Rosten. Copyright © 1985 by Leo Rosten. All rights reserved. Reprinted by permission of Crown Publishers, Inc. Reprinted by permission of the William Morris Agency,Inc. on behalf of the Author Copyright © 1985 by Leo Rosten

SOAP CORRESPONDENCE from A HOTEL IS A PLACE by Shelley Berman. Reprinted by permission of the Putnam Publishing Group/Price Stern Sloan, In. From A Hotel Is A Place by Shelley Berman. Copyright © Shelley Berman.

John Long's Campfire Howlers

Copyright © 1994 by John Long

10 9 8 7 6 5 4 3 2 1

All rights reserved, including the right to reproduce this book or portions thereof in any form or by any means, electronic or mechanical, including photocopying and recording, unless authorization is obtained, in writing, from the publisher. Inquiries should be addressed to ICS BOOKS, 1370 E. 86th Place, Merrillville, IN 46410.

Printed in U.S.A.

All ICS titles are printed on 50% recycled paper from pre-consumer waste.

All sheets are processed without using acid.

Published By:
ICS BOOKS, Inc., 1370 E. 86th Place, Merrillville, IN 46410. 800-541-7323

Co-Published in Canada By:
Vanwell Publishing Ltd., 1 Northrop Crescent, St. Catharines, Ontario L2M 6P5. 800-661-6136.

Library of Congress Cataloging-in-Publication Data

Campfire Howlers / edited by John Long.

p. cm.

ISBN: 1-57034-000-5

1. Literature–Collections. 2. Storytelling. I. Long, John, 1954— .

PN6014.C275 1994 94-12380

808.83'1—dc20 CIP

Table of Contents

Introduction	IV
Truth In Advertising	1
Anti-Semitism	6
My Friend Phil	7
Miss Oyster	18
Tushmaker's Toothpullerby	19
Rabbi Rosenbloom	22
Cloudland Revisited	23
Girlfriend	28
The Dirty Nincompoop Who Edits that Journal	29
The Story Of The Old Ram	33
Lectures On Astronomy	39
IBM Sent This?	48
The Latest Improvements In Artillery	49
Beautiful Girl	52
Third World Driving	53
He Quit Snoring	58
Jud Brownin Hears Ruby Play	59
Budding Actor	64
King Kong Comes To Wabag	65
The Three Wishes	70
No Time For Sergeants	71
From: A Double-Barrelled Detective Story	85
The First Piano In A Mining Camp	89
You Drive, Dear	97
Parisian Shave	101
Somebody In My Bed	104
Kindly Dig Your Grave	105
Gambling	120
Fenimore Cooper's Literary Offenses	121
So What?	126
The Road To Miltown	127
Voltaire	133
A Real Man	144
Turkish Bath	145
What To Do With All Those Free Soaps When Traveling	150

Introduction

Most of us throw on a pack and head into the wilderness not only to affirm our connection to the natural world, but also to harmonize the discord in our life. Comedy is a great harmonizer as well. Some call it a survival mechanism. Much has been written about humor, but we can no more analyze a piece of humor and discover its secret than we can saw a saxophone in half and discover a Coltrane solo.

Humor comes in varied clothes, but quality material often has some truth sewn into it. The gag, however, is invariably just calisthenics with words. The burlesque is sometimes hilarious, and the "dumb" anecdote priceless if it's transcendentally stupid and guileless, like Bennett Cerf's *Miss Oyster*. But a mean-spirited or nasty tale is offensive and hateful, which points up the shape of a lot of modern "comedy." Troll back through the golden age of American humor—roughly from 1840 to the turn of the twentieth century—and see how much of modern comedy has prattled itself into punch lines and jokesmithing. The old material is dated, yes, but while many of the details are either quaint or long gone (like mining camps and flintlock rifles), the human being hasn't changed one bit. Because the old material gives us a different and forgotten angle on things, the old can in fact become the new.

That much said, superior modern humor does exist, but with the glut of electronic media, much of it is performed in the first instance, and read only as a secondary diversion, if at all. Particularly with shorter vignettes and scenarios, much of the magic is in the oration itself, and you can't reduce it completely to writing any more than you can play a streak of lightning on an electric guitar. A lot depends on the delivery.

In compiling this volume I skimmed dozens of anthologies and collections. It was obvious from the start that the world didn't need another joke book (none of which could hold my attention), so I focused instead on stories, believing they show more skill and insight. Short bits were sought to bridge the longer pieces, and were included only if they struck me as unique.

The material in *Campfire Howlers* is of different types and from different times. Some pieces might be unsuitable for kids, but adults should feel right in the saddle. A campfire book always serves two purposes: it must be a storytelling resource for the fireside, and a refuge during tedious plane rides, when we're trapped inside a tent during a storm, and so on. To this end, I've included half a dozen longer pieces.

A few of the shorter pieces were taken from collections that featured virtually thousands of entries, and sometimes no authorship was given. It's criminal to feature work and not have a name to hang on it, but more so, I think, to let a great morsel die because it came to you anonymously.

I hope this material will light up your world as it does mine everytime I read it. The large typeface should ease the task when the conditions are poor or the fire is running low.

—*John Long,*
Valencia, Venezuela

Truth in Advertising
by Henri Beard

Acting in a spirit of new-found militancy, the Federal Trade Commission recently stiffened its regulations covering advertising to require advertisers to refrain from making claims, demonstrations, dramatizations, broad comparisons or statistical statements involving their products that they are not prepared to instantly substantiate when requested to do so by the commission. The possibility that the new FTC rules will actually convince advertisers to tell the truth is so unsettling that we are offering, as a public service, three examples of what an honest commercial might be like, to prevent the inevitable onset of mass hysteria should one ever appear.

• • •

(*A kitchen. It could be anywhere, but is, in fact, in the studio of a major network. In the sink, on either side of the drain, lurk two stains the size of veal cutlets. The doorbell rings and a comely homemaker admits a well-known female plumber.*)

JOSEPHINE: Hi there, Mrs. Waxwell. Say, that sink looks like the scuppers of a frigate. Where did those stains come from anyway?

MRS. WAXWELL: Oh, the man from the advertising agency put them there. Actually, they're just poster paint. But they are identical. He used a micrometer.

JOSEPHINE: Well, this looks like a job for new, improved Cosmic, which differs from old Cosmic in that its frankly deceptive container is made from aluminum, whereas its predecessor was composed of cheesy old steel.

MRS. WAXWELL: Cosmic? Why not this can of ordinary rock salt which one of the stagehands has labeled "Another Household Cleanser?"

JOSEPHINE: I'll tell you why! Because only Cosmic contains Chloaxo, A Beaver Bros. trade name for certain tar globules added chiefly for bulk. Tell you what, let's try your cleanser against new Cosmic, to which, for purposes of this demonstration, lye, potassium, formic acid and iron filings have been added. You put yours on that stain, and I'll put Cosmic on this one.

MRS. WAXWELL: Due to an arthritic condition, I will be unable to muster much more scrubbing force than that of a healthy fly.

JOSEPHINE: That's all right, just sort of swish it around while I grind in Cosmic with the powerful right hand I developed pitching horseshoes and juggling sash weights. There! Now let's rinse and see which cleanser did better.

MRS. WAXWELL: Gosh, Cosmic even pitted the porcelain, while my disappointing, slug-a-bed cleanser just sat there and fizzed! If in my real life I ever got closer to a kitchen than the Mariner 7 space probe did to Mars, I'd switch to Cosmic in a trice!

JOSEPHINE: Though not in reality a licensed plumber, I must say that such a move would seem to be indicated!

• • •

(*A pair of children, one each of the two leading sexes, are poised around a pet's dish, into which Mom is pouring something that looks a lot like shrapnel.*)

JUNIOR: Gee, Ma, I sure hope Muffin likes these Kitty-Krunchies. He sure must be hungry!

MOM: And no wonder, considering his incarceration in a prop trunk backstage since last Wednesday.

SIS: Say, why do cats crave Kitty-Krunchies? Is it due to the thin coating of a habit-forming drug that overrides the animal's natural revulsion to these otherwise tasteless nuggets of pressed cellulose and fly ash, or could it be the powerful feline hormones added to each and every pellet by the manufacturer to unhinge their instincts?

JUNIOR: Maybe it's their eatability. After all, these bite-size chunks pass right through kitty's digestive system like water through a goose, then emerge as an easily disposable, odorless slime that keeps kitty's box as fresh and sweet-smelling!

MOM: Yes, and unlike other cat foods, which contain chalky cereals and lumps of unhealthy meat, Kitty-Krunchies are laced with common gravel, which gives cats the heft and stability they need to stay in one place. And what's more, when submitted to a panel of distinguished veterinarians, Kitty-Krunchies were preferred two-to-one over an alternate diet consisting of a leading spot remover and ground glass.

SIS: Here comes Muffin now! Wow, look at him pack away those Kitty-Krunchies!

JUNIOR: Golly, Ma, let's get all the great Kitty-Krunchies gourmet dinners! There are more than eight to choose from, and although the taste-tempting treat illustrated in full color on the outside of the box bears no relation whatsoever to its contents, each one is doused liberally with a different colored lead-based paint to perk up puss's flagging interest!

MOM: That's right, and Kitty-Krunchies cost only pennies a serving, or, if you have no pennies, two quarters and a dime. Get Kitty-Krunchies today!

• • •

(*A teenager's room. Plenty of pennants, five guitars, and a toss pillow imprinted with a road sign. Bob is in a funk as Ted enters.*)

TED: Going to the dance on Saturday night, Bob? All the gang will be there.

BOB: Aw, I can't, Ted. As these daubs of red stage paint on my face are intended to indicate, I've broken out in hundreds of repulsive pimples. I just can't let the gang see me like this.

TED: Well, Bob, doctors know that the prime cause of acne is enlarged pores, and, say, yours look big enough to plant shrubs in. What you need is Dermathex, the inert jellylike substance that separates the men from the boils and makes carbuncles cry "uncle." Here, I just happen to have a tube of the aforementioned preparation in my chinos.

BOB: How does it work?

TED: Frankly, Bob, a scientific study conducted recently at a major university showed that it doesn't, but then, who trusts a bunch of ivory-tower longhairs, anyway?

BOB: But isn't it just another cover-up cream?

TED: Of course, but why not give it a try? All you have to do is rub it into affected regions. Then, as soon as Dermathex strikes your skin, your facial lymph glands—your body's first line of defense—will slam shut your pores rather than permit the many toxins Dermathex contains to penetrate any deeper. With any luck, once you've managed to remove the tough screen Dermathex provides, your pimples will have packed their bags.

BOB: Hell, I'll try anything.

(*That Saturday*)

TED: Hey, Bob, how about that dance?

BOB: You bet! Since my entire face is now raw as a flank steak, I can say I just fell asleep under the sun lamp. The gang will never know the difference!

TED: Dermathex, it's better than nothing!

ANTI-SEMITISM

Mrs. Chauncey Ashley III telephoned the headquarters of the infantry base near Great Oaks, her ancestral home. "This is Mrs. Chauncey Ashley the Third, and with Thanksgiving coming up, I thought it would be nice for us to have ten of your fine enlisted men share our family feast."

"That's very kind of you, Mrs. Ashley."

"There's only one thing—I'm sure you understand: my husband and I prefer not to have any Jews."

"Madam, I quite understand."

When her front doorbell rang on Thanksgiving Day, Mrs. Ashley, dressed to the nines, hurried to the door herself. She flung it open. "Welcome to Great—" She stopped, aghast.

Under the great portico stood ten smiling black soldiers.

"Omigod," gasped Mrs. Ashley. "There has been a terrible mistake."

The black sergeant said, "Oh no, ma'am. Captain Finkelstein never makes a mistake."

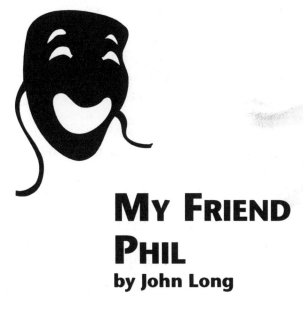

My Friend Phil
by John Long

For the half-dozen years before Paraguay's Rio Caiman swept him away from us (along with his two kayaking partners, Marty Silver and Rick Navarro), the adventure community was divided into two camps: those who had been with Davenport, and those who had not. Philip and I had been together since the trouble years before the world had ever heard of Philip Randolph Davenport.

The Davenport family was from another planet, or so thought my father, an Aspen carpenter who had built the deck on the Davenports' summer home near Ajax Mountain. The home, a palatial article set on a hillside overlooking Golden Butte, was a curious amalgam of Manhattan chic and aboriginal Peru, and suggested the eccentric union of the Davenports themselves.

Herbert Davenport was a kook gentleman anthropologist who had spent nearly twenty years studying antique cultures deep in the Peruvian rain forest. Katherine Putnam Davenport was a bejeweled, vinegary former debutante with a tongue like a carving knife. She was the kind that didn't go out in the sun without an umbrella. Her husband had been so long out of circulation that when he returned to the States from the jungle, he was unfit, if not incapable, of any legitimate work. Katherine's tacit agreement with the Davenport patriarchs was that as long as she kept her husband on the sidelines, where he couldn't embarrass anyone, their ration of the enormous family fortune was secure.

For more than fifteen years Katherine and Herbert had seen one another only at Christmas and for a few weeks each summer. When phlebitis finally drove Herbert from the rain forest for good (along with Philip, who had spent most of his childhood with his father in Peru), he and Katherine were like strangers thrown together. But Herbert was lost in the civilized world without his wife's direction, and she was hopeless without his money. For the first year they tolerated each other in a curious, aristocratic kind of way. After another year they were an inseparable odd couple.

The Davenports spent their summers in Aspen, where Philip and I had both been in my uncle's Explorer Scout troop and fell in together. When the family invited me to join them for a week at their casita near La Paz, Baja California, my folks thought it a wise plan, since I was nearly sixteen and had never left Colorado. Philip was rather wild, and his folks were from Mars, but they were respectable and monied, and if anything should happen, Dad figured they could get me back to Aspen soon enough.

The casita belonged to Herbert's brother, Harold, who had spent a bundle trimming it out, and used it once every couple of years or not at all. A couple hundred yards below the paved road leading to La Paz, and close by the sea, lay a hard-packed dirt road crowded with dog carts; kids on rusty bicycles; women with black rebozos pulled over their shoulders dragging wailing infants by the hand; and peons with great loads of firewood on their bare shoulders trudging toward the charcoal factory in town. Just off this dirt road, set back in a copse of green bamboo, was the casita—a diamond in the rough if ever I saw one.

Set up on creaky oak pylons, the three-bedroom house cantilevered over gulf waters famous for sportfishing. The exterior was plain, but the interior was tooled out for pseudo-Mexican gentry, with portraits of Cantinflas and Pedro Infante and a few San Sebastian bullfighters on the reed walls; silver-trimmed wicker furniture covered with combed hides on the wooden floor; and a collection of priceless Spanish glassware and Toltec artifacts in filigreed cabinets against the den walls. A silver horseshoe hung over the kitchen door for luck.

Katherine Davenport hated the place the minute we got there. Never mind the decor: ruffians prowled the dirt road just beyond the front door, the electricity was off and on, mostly off, the humidity was terminal, and the flooring was so warped in spots that she could see the anxious ocean through the gaps.

On the second night, while Phil and I were swinging face down in hammocks and trying to spit through the rifts in the floor, Mrs. Davenport let out a scream that could have frozen mescal. A cucaracha the size of a taquito had scampered across her bedspread, and several fiddler crabs had made their way into the bedroom as well. She swore she wouldn't stay in that house one second longer. Pop Davenport loaded up the rental Jeep and took his wife to the Hotel Hidalgo, a five-star lodging in town. We could come if we wanted to. We didn't. Pop Davenport would swing by in the morning to take us out for breakfast. The Jeep wheeled off, and we were alone.

Philip rifled the liquor cabinet and came away with a bottle of Jose Cuervo Gold. We moved to the back of the house and a warped plank staircase—barely eight feet wide and set between two rotting pylons—that spilled from the den straight into the sea, where a small, frail-looking dinghy was tethered. We sat on the last step with our legs in salt water and gazed out over the moon-rinsed gulf, talking about climbing the Maroon Bells back in Aspen, and maybe doing some bull riding here in La Paz—if we could find a bull. The tequila clobbered us, burning all the way down to our toes.

The bottle was only a fourth gone when we spotted a giant cutlass carving through the water, flashing like mother-of-pearl as it swiveled into the moonlight. "Shark," Philip whispered.

I bounded up a couple of stairs to a pylon as Philip jumped into the dinghy, snatched an oar and started bashing the water. "Frenzied movements attract them," Philip cried, beating away. "I read it in Argosy."

"Attract them?" I yelled, clinging to the pylon. "Jesus, Phil. That fin's big as a STOP sign. You sure you wanna be fuckin' with it?" Phil thrashed the water even harder. I moved to the top step as the fin swept close by the dinghy, circled under the house and plowed back into the deep. Philip jumped from the dinghy, splashed up the stairs and into the house, then returned with the remains of our chicken dinner, chumming the water with bones and necks and gizzards. Several times the gleaming fin cruised past, but never as close as the first time.

"Blood," Philip said angrily. "We need blood." And he hurled the tequila bottle into the sea.

It was nearly dawn before I could drift off in my hammock, picturing that great fin circling under the bedroom floor. When I woke the next morning I found Philip in the kitchen, studying the big silver horseshoe hanging above the door. Pop Davenport had already come and gone, and Philip showed me a thick wad of peso notes to prove it. His mom had a fever and his father didn't want to leave her alone in the hotel. We would have to fetch our own breakfast.

Philip reached up above the doorjamb and yanked the horseshoe free from its nails, his eyes burning. "We're going fishing, Jim."

We jogged up to the main road, hailed an *autobus* and were soon scudding around central La Paz, grabbing a *cocktail de camarones* in one stall, ogling the senoritas in others. We found an old man, hunched over a foot-powered grinder, who milled one end of the silver horseshoe into a pick, sharp as fate. I watched the fury of peso notes changing hands, Philip rattling off *espanol* like a native. Smoking lung-busting *Delicados, sin filtros*, we hustled on through the fish market, ankle deep in mullet offal. At another stall a fleshy woman, her cavernous cleavage dusted with talc, cut ten feet of thick chain off a gigantic, rusty spool. "For leader," said Philip, grabbing my arm and racing off. From another lady in a booth hung with crocheted murals of Jesus Christo, Philip bought 200 yards of 500-kilo-test polypropylene rope. Meanwhile, her husband welded the chain leader onto the sharpened horseshoe, sparks from the acetylene rig raining over Jesus like shooting stars.

"Now for the bait."

We took a cab to the slaughterhouse on the edge of town. Outside the reeking, sheet-metal structure, Philip waved through a curtain of flies and stopped an Indian girl, maybe sixteen. Her hair was pulled back in thick black braids framing a face so striking that armadillos raced up my spine just looking at her. She was selling fried pork rinds and sweetbreads, and when Philip asked her a probing question, she killed him with her eyes. Philip talked some more, cajoling her. I understood nothing of their machine-gun Spanish. Slowly, the girl's glare melted into a snigger. When Phil's hand went out with a ten-peso note, she reached for it quick as a frog's tongue. But not quick enough. Philip shook his head, flashing a wily smile and holding the bill out of reach. She answered his smile with a sly one of her own, glanced around at empty streets, then quickly hiked up her white muslin blouse, and for about one-thousandth of a second my eyes feasted on two perfect brown globes crowned with two perky, pinto bean-like nipples. Then her shirt was back down and the bill was gone from Philip's hand and she was two golden heels hot-footing to some shady nook to admire the *gringo* boy's money.

"I'd marry her in a second," Phil said, "if I was old enough."

We took a bus back to the casita, laden with a giant bull's heart wrapped in brown paper and twine and a bucket of red slop so heavy it put my hand to sleep carrying it.

On the stairs behind the house Phil baited the sharpened horseshoe with the ruby-colored bull's heart, duct-taped a soccer ball to the chain leader just below where he'd tied on the polypropylene rope, then neatly coiled the rope on the stairs and lashed the free end 'round one of the creaky pylons. As he hefted the bucket of entrails into the dinghy, my balls shriveled to the merest garbanzos.

"You can either watch the line here in the bow, or row. You pick."

"I thought we were going to just chuck the thing in from here," I said.

"Shark won't go for it. You saw how he shied away last night. And anyway, I bought all this rope."

Two hundred yards of new rope seemed a poor excuse to row into shark-infested waters in a leaky dinghy full of blood and guts, but Phil was already in the boat yelling, "Come on, Jim. It's a two-minute job."

I took the oars and rowed straight out into the gulf, my limbs trembling so horribly I could barely pull. The dinghy was overloaded and tippy as hell and several geysers spewed up through cracks in the flexing hull. I watched the house slowly recede, the line slithering out from its coil. My chest heaved, and I felt the water rise to ankle level around my tennis shoes.

Fifty yards out, Phil tossed the bucket of gore overboard and a dull red ring bled out around us.

"That sucker's any closer than Acapulco, he'll smell this," he said. "Believe it."

"I do."

Phil hurled the big red heart overboard with a plunk, the weight yanking out the chain leader, which chattered over the low gunwale of the dinghy. The soccer ball shot out and sank. Phil panned the flat blue plane for a moment. Then the ball popped up near us, the waters churned and he screamed, "Put your back into it, Jim, or we're goners!"

I heaved at the oars, my heart thundering in my ears and my lungs gasping down mouthfuls of air, the dinghy fairly hydroplaning, Phil bailing furiously with the bucket and screaming, "Pull, man, pull." I pulled harder and faster, trying to retrace the polypropylene line floating on the water, marking the way back home. The flimsy oars bent horribly as Phil screamed to go faster and faster, till they were driving like bee's wings. Twenty yards from the house we were both screaming, breathless and terrified, the water in the dinghy shin deep, sinking by the second. A final heave and I powered right into the stairs; the dinghy buckled and split in half, dumping us into carnivorous waters. We splashed and groped for the stairs, then stampeded over each other and through the house and out the front door, puking saltwater and howling, finally collapsing in front of a man selling shaved ice from a pushcart.

Phil lay in the dirt, breathing hard and feigning palsy, his face screwed up and his eyes rolled back in his head. I laughed so fearfully and so hard my stomach turned inside out.

"Not that we're afraid to die or anything," Phil gasped.

The man with the pushcart couldn't have looked more astonished if he'd seen a burro prance by on its hind legs.

After a few minutes we stole back into the house, tiptoeing a step at a time through the hall, through the narrow den, past the wall of glassware and artifacts, pausing at the open door and the stairs below and staring out over the gulf at the line sleeping on the surface and the soccer ball bobbing peacefully fifty yards away. There wasn't so much as a crawfish on the line. Never had been.

"Chickenshit shark," Phil mumbled. And we sat down.

For several hours we sat hip to hip on the stairs, gazing out at the bobbing ball so hard that the flat horizon and the heat of high noon put us in a trance. Then everything was quiet. Too quiet.

"Wonder where the gulls went?" I asked, dizzy with the tension.

The rope suddenly jumped out of the water, the staircase groaned, and splinters flew off the pylon as the line lashed itself taut as a bowstring.

"He's hooked," cried Phil.

We leaped up and grabbed the rope as the old pylon bowed against the stairs. Rusty nails sprang up from fractured planks and sand crabs scurried out from dark places. Far out on the water we saw an invincible fin, a mad roil of water and then we heard a jagged snap. A scythe-shaped tail curled on itself and the rope went slack against the pylon. A gathering surge was tearing straight toward us, looking like a submarine surfacing as the line doubled back on itself. Close to us, the fin swerved suddenly and headed out to open sea. We couldn't appreciate the monster's speed till we noticed the loose line, straightening as fast as if lashed to a cigarette boat.

"Grab the rope, or the house is going with him," Phil yelled, lunging for the line.

There was no checking the creature, but I stupidly grabbed the rope anyway. The shark hit the slack line, wrenching me straight off the stairs and into the playground of the blazing gray terror. I furiously crabbing from the water and up the stairs, and didn't stop running till the den. And there I stood, bloody and wheezing, dripping saltwater onto a nineteenth-century Malagan rug. I was dry before I staggered back to the fray.

The line was slack, then taut. Then slack again. We pulled. Phil cussed like a sailor. The rope smoked through my raw hands. I wanted to cry. We pulled some more.

After an hour we'd gained a little. With the rope doubled 'round a pylon, there was just enough friction that we could lock the beast off—even gain some rope when the tension eased for a second. After two hours we'd reeled the creature a quarter of the way in. Several times it broke the surface, obsidian eyes glinting in the sun. The line under my hands dripped red, and the saltwater tortured the grooves seared into my palms. The more line we gained, the fiercer the combat. The monster would relax for a moment and we'd win a yard, then the line would twang tight, the pylon would creak, and the remaining stairs would shudder under our bicycling feet. It was close to a standoff.

"We need help," Phil said. "Lock him off for a minute."

I braced against the pylon and held fast as the house behind me filled with dark-haired boys, street urchins, and even the man with the pushcart, snagged from the dirt road just outside. When the line went momentarily slack, Philip unwound it from the pylon and, racing against time, ran the rope in a straight line from the water up the stairs and through the den, down the hall and right out the front door. The brown crowd turned its back on the casita, each man and boy clasping the rope over the shoulder, Philip yelling, "Hale, hale, hooooooombres." The tug-of-war was on, with "Tiburon, tiburon grandote" yelled over and over like a chant at a soccer match.

Philip joined me on the crumbling stairs, hauling hand over hand now, the whole gulf one huge swell coursing toward us, quickly becoming a shark as big as a four-man bobsled, thrashing against the straining rope.

"Let off," I yelled, releasing the line and backpedaling away. "Tell them to let off."

But it was no good. The gathering crowd was already fifty feet past the front door, their feet churning the dust. Phil and I jumped to a pylon when, with one titanic lurch, they hauled the opalescent monster to light. It flopped bodylong onto the buckling stairs, the silver horseshoe hooked deep through its toothy lower jaw, the line taut as a guywire. The beast did a move from the deep, lurched a yard straight up off the stairs and, now airborne, was yanked right past us. Its bear-trap maw snapped and a sandpaper flank rasped the skin off my arm as he jackknifed over the stairs, through the open back door and into the den, a place of leisure and filigreed cabinets, of rum toddies and ripe mangos, of drowsy vacation afternoons. Another move from ten fathoms and he clipped the legs out from under the rosewood and ivory table.

"Let off, for Christ's sake," I screamed from the stairs. "Let it go."

But every able man for five miles along the dirt road must have been latched onto that rope, and all fifty of them were hauling for pride and country: cabbies, rummies, men in white suits and wrap-around shades, a priest in huaraches, and nine National Guardsmen yelling commands and tapping slackers with batons. But 900 pounds of shark wasn't going easily. A smashing tail, and the cabinets were gone, the Toltec artifacts were so many shards, the Spanish glassware, sand. Colossal teeth shredded filigreed wood, ripped the hides off wicker chairs. A flip and a twirl and he unraveled the Malagan rug. The heaving crowd dragged the monster further through the narrow den. Rich purple blood splattered over bright white walls. A deep-water kip, an airborne nosebutt—and a wall caved in. Salt-rotted wood fractured and floor slats snapped to attention as the ceiling dropped a yard and parted to show a splintered smile of blue Mexican sky.

And the brown mob pulled. The great monster died ten times, then lurched back to life, marking its passage through the open house by knocking sheetrock off the hallway walls, murdering the grandfather clock, blasting the front door off its hinges.

At last the noble creature lay outside, its hornblende eyes locked on infinity, its jagged mouth open. One of the National Guardsmen probed the cavity with his baton, and in a final show of sea force, the huge mouth snapped shut. The guardsman jumped back with a hickory stub in his hand, yelling, "Hijo de puta."

For nearly an hour we all stood around in a daze, staring at the great monster as kids prodded it with long sticks and several policemen posed for pictures taken with an antique Kodak Brownie Philip swore had no film in it.

Word of the conquest spread down the dirt road like a whirlwind, and shortly, a flatbed truck from the fish market sputtered up. The beast was logrolled onto the lift and then into the bed of the truck. In five more minutes the shark was a relic of memory. The gathered crowd slowly went their way, thumping each other's back, and we were once again alone.

I was grated raw, rope burned, sunburned, splintered, bloodied and spent, my trunks and shirt in tatters, one tennis shoe gone, my hands two oozing, pulpy knobs. Philip was completely unmarked. His shirt was still tucked in. But the casita couldn't have been more trashed had we trapped a grizzly inside it for two weeks—without food or water.

We tried a hundred different lies on each other but couldn't concoct an excuse as big as that shark. Finally, Philip went to the Hotel Hidalgo to try to explain; and in an example of his transcendental luck, he found his parents preparing to leave on the next plane for the States. His mother thought another night in Mexico might kill her. Without reservations, they were able to secure only two seats on the 4:50 Air Mexicana flight to Los Angeles; but Pop Davenport had booked us on the 6:30 flight that same night. The Davenports would wait for us at the airport in L.A., and we'd all go to Disneyland.

Philip raced back to the casita and, after wandering through the ruins, said, "We've got to torch it."

"Torch it?" I asked.

"Yeah, burn it down."

I pictured myself in a Mexican jail. Forever.

"You want to try and explain this?" Philip laughed, glancing at the ocean through a ten-foot hole in the floor, then up through the rent in the roof. "This joint's dusted."

"How do we explain the fire?" I asked.

"We don't," Philip smiled. "That's the beauty of it. It burns down after we're gone. And it will."

Philip shagged into town, returned with a cab, a gallon of kerosene and two votive candles. We threw our suitcases into the cab waiting on the dirt road, then Philip soaked the den floor with the kerosene, planted two candles in the middle of the buckled floor, lit them, walked out the open door and into the cab, and we were off.

As we ground up off the tarmac, we spotted a plume of black smoke out east, rising off the fringe of the ocean. Philip leaned back in his seat and said, "Wonder how long that sucker was?"

When Harold Davenport returned to Mexico two years later, he found two shrimp boats tied up to the blackened pylons where his vacation home had once stood. Nobody seemed to know how the fire had started. Or even when.

MISS OYSTER
by Bennett Cerf

The oysters found a fine new bed several miles up the Sound, and were happily packing their belongings—all except little Mary Oyster, who sat sobbing bitterly in a corner. "What's the matter?" asked her father anxiously. "We'll have a wonderful new home. There's nothing to cry about." "Oh yes there is," wailed Mary. "Johnny Bass will never be able to find me now, and I love him with all my heart." "But does Johnny Bass reciprocate your devotion?" inquired the parent. "Indeed he does," Mary assured him. "Last night he took me in his arms at the end of the pier out there. First he kissed me here on the forehead. Then he kissed me here on the lips. And then—my God, *my pearl!*"

Tushmaker's Toothpullerby
by John Phoenix
(George H. Derby)

Dr. Tushmaker was never regularly bred as a physician or surgeon, but he possessed naturally a strong mechanical genius and a fine appetite; and finding his teeth of great service in gratifying the latter propensity, he concluded that he could do more good in the world, and create more real happiness therein, by putting the teeth of its inhabitants in good order, than in any other way; so Tushmaker became a dentist. He was the man that first invented the method of placing small cog-wheels in the back teeth for the more perfect mastication of food, and he claimed to be the original discoverer of that method of filling cavities with a kind of putty, which, becoming hard directly, causes the tooth to ache so grievously that it has to be pulled, thereby giving the dentist two successive fees for the same job. Tushmaker was one day seated in his office, in the city of Boston, Massachusetts, when a stout old fellow, named Byles, presented himself to have a back tooth drawn. The dentist seated his patient in the chair of torture, and, opening his mouth, discovered there an enormous tooth, on the right hand side, about as large, as he afterwards expressed it, "as a small Polyglot Bible." I shall have trouble with this tooth, thought Tushmaker, but he clapped on his heaviest forceps, and pulled. It didn't come. Then he tried the turn-screw, exerting his utmost strength, but the tooth wouldn't stir. "Go away from here," said Tushmaker to Byles, "and return in a week, and I'll draw that tooth for you, or know the reason why." Byles got up, clapped a handkerchief to his jaw, and put forth. Then the dentist went to work, and in three days he invented an instrument which he was confident would pull anything. It was a combination of the lever, pulley, wheel and axle, inclined plane, wedge and screw. The castings were made, and the machine put up in the office, over an iron chair rendered perfectly stationary by iron rods going down into the foundations of the granite building. In a week old Byles returned; he was clamped into the iron chair, the forceps connected with the machine attached firmly to the tooth, and Tushmaker, stationing himself in the rear, took hold of a lever four feet in length. He turned slightly. Old Byles gave a groan and lifted his right leg. Another turn; another groan, and up went the leg again. "What do you raise your leg for?" asked the doctor. "I can't help it," said the patient. "Well," rejoined Tushmaker, "that tooth is bound to come out now."

He turned the lever clear round with a sudden jerk, and snapped old Byle's head clean and clear from his shoulders, leaving a space of four inches between the severed parts! They had a *post-mortem* examination—the roots of the tooth were found extending down the right side, through the right leg, and turning up in two prongs under the sole of the right foot! "No wonder," said Tushmaker, "he raised his right leg." The jury thought so too, but they found the roots much decayed; and five surgeons swearing that mortification would have ensued in a few months, Tushmaker was cleared on a verdict of "justifiable homicide." He was a little shy of that instrument for some time afterward; but one day an old lady, feeble and flaccid, came in to have a tooth drawn, and thinking it would come out very easy, Tushmaker concluded, just by way of variety, to try the machine. He did so, and at the first turn drew the old lady's skeleton completely and entirely from her body, leaving her a mass of quivering jelly in her chair! Tushmaker took her home in a pillow-case. She lived seven years after that, and they called her the "India-Rubber Woman." She had suffered terribly with the rheumatism, but after this occurrence, never had a pain in her bones. The dentist kept them in a glass case. After this, the machine was sold to the contractor of the Boston Customhouse, and it was found that a child of three years of age could, by a single turn of the screw, raise a stone weighing twenty-three tons. Smaller ones were made on the same principle, and sold to the keepers of hotels and restaurants. They were used for boning turkeys. There is no moral to this story whatever, and it is possible that a few details may have become slightly exaggerated. Of course, there can be no doubt of the truth of the main incidents.

RABBI ROSENBLOOM
from Feldman's Cache

Three rowboats moved along the totally flooded streets, and the water was still rising as the torrent from heaven raged unabated. The rescuers spied a strange figure on the roof of a small building: a tall, bearded man, wearing a wide, flat black hat, his arms crossed.

"Come down!" shouted the rowers. "Get into the boat!"

The tall figure gestured calmly. "Save others. Do not worry about me. I am Rabbi Gershon Rosenbloom. The Lord will save me!"

An hour later, another boat—this one with an outboard motor—approached. "Hey! You on the roof! Come down! The waters are still rising!"

The rabbi, standing cross-armed despite water up to his waist, called out, "*Go on!* Save others. I am a rabbi. I have complete faith in my Lord!"

And an hour later, the rains still pouring down, a helicopter searching for survivors of the flood hovered over the rabbi, lowered its ladder, the pilot's voice bellowing from a bullhorn: "Grab the ladder, man! The water's up to your chin! This is your last—"

"Fear not!" sang the rabbi. "I am a man of God! And—He—will—*glub, glub, kmpf* . . ." And Rabbi Gershon Rosenbloom, that good and faithful servant of the Lord, sank beneath the rising waters.

Being a soul of the utmost virtue, without stain throughout his life, the rabbi, within an instant after drowning, found himself among the Heavenly Throng, gazing at the effulgent radiance of God Himself.

"Oh, Lord!" cried the rabbi. "How *could* You? I had absolute faith in You, and You let me drown! How could you let me down—"

"'Let you *down?*'" bridled the Lord. "I sent two boats and a helicopter to take you off that roof, you idiot!"

Cloudland Revisited
by S.J. Perelman

Some weeks ago, rummaging through the film library of the Museum of Modern Art, I discovered among its goodies a print of the very production of *Twenty Thousand Leagues* that had mesmerized me in 1916, and, by ceaseless nagging, bedeviled the indulgent custodians into screening it for me. Within twenty minutes, I realized that I was watching one of the really great cinema nightmares, a *cauchemar* beside which *King Kong, The Tiger Man,* and *The Cat People* were as staid as so many quilting bees.

The premise of *Twenty Thousand Leagues,* in a series of quick nutshells, is that the Navy, dismayed by reports of a gigantic sea serpent preying on our merchant marine, dispatches an expedition to exterminate it. Included in the party are Professor Aronnax, a French scientist with luxuriant crepe hair and heavy eye make-up who looks like a phrenologist out of the funny papers; his daughter, a kittenish ingenue all corkscrew curls and maidenly simpers; and the latter's heartbeat, a broth of a boy identified as Ned Land, Prince of Harpooners. Their quarry proves, of course, to be the submarine *Nautilus,* commanded by the redoubtable Captain Nemo, which sinks their vessel and takes them prisoner. Nemo is Melville's Captain Ahab with French dressing, as bizarre a mariner as ever trod on a weevil. He has a profile like Garibaldi's, set off by a white goatee; wears a Santa Claus suit and a turban made out of a huck towel; and smokes a church warden pipe. Most submarine commanders, as a rule, busy themselves checking gauges and twiddling the periscope, but Nemo spends all his time smiting his forehead and vowing revenge, though on whom it is not clear. The decor of the *Nautilus,* obviously inspired by a Turkish bordello, is pure early Matisse; Oriental rugs, hassocks, and mother-of-pearl taborets abound, and in one shot I thought I detected a parlor floor lamp with a fringed shade, which must have been a problem in dirty weather. In all justice, however, Paton's conception of a submarine interior was no more florid than Jules Verne's. Among the ship's accouterments, I find on consulting the great romancer, he lists a library containing twelve thousand volumes, a dining room with oak sideboards, and a thirty-foot drawing room full of Old Masters, tapestry, and sculpture.

Apparently, the front office figured that so straightforward a narrative would never be credible, because complications now really begin piling up. "About this time," a subtitle announces, "Lieutenant Bond and four Union Army scouts, frustrated in an attempt to destroy their balloon, are carried out to sea." A long and murky sequence full of lightning, falling sandbags, and disheveled character actors occupies the next few minutes, the upshot being that the cloud-borne quintet is stranded on a remote key called Mysterious Island. One of its more mysterious aspects is an unchaperoned young person in a leopard-skin sarong who dwells in the trees and mutters gibberish to herself. The castaways find this tropical Ophelia in a pit they have dug to ward off prowling beasts, and Lieutenant Bond, who obviously has been out of touch with women since he was weaned, loses his heart to her. To achieve greater obscurity, the foregoing is intercut with limitless footage of Captain Nemo and his hostages goggling at the wonders of the deep through a window in the side of the submarine. What they see is approximately what anybody might who has quaffed too much "shine" and is peering into a home aquarium, but, after all, tedium is a relative matter. When you come right down to it, a closeup of scup feeding around a coral arch is no more static than one of Robert Taylor.

At this juncture, a completely new element enters the plot to further befuddle it, in the form of one Charles Denver, "a retired ocean trader in a distant land." Twelve years earlier, a flashback reveals, Denver had got a skinful of lager and tried to ravish an Indian maharanee called Princess Daaker. The lady had thereupon plunged a dagger into her thorax, and Denver, possibly finding the furniture too heavy, had stolen her eight-year-old daughter. We see him now in a mood of remorse approaching that of Macbeth, drunkenly clawing his collar and reviling the phantoms that plague him—one of them, by the way, a rather engaging Mephistopheles of the sort depicted in advertisements for quick-drying varnish. To avoid losing his mind, the trader boards his yacht and sets off for Mysterious Island, a very peculiar choice indeed, for if ever there was a convocation of loons anywhere, it is there. Captain Nemo is fluthering around in the lagoon, wrestling with an inflated rubber octopus; Lieutenant Bond and the leopard girl (who it presently emerges, is Princess Daaker's daughter, left there to die) are spooning on the cliffs; and just to enliven things, one of Bond's scouts is planning to supplant him as leader and abduct the maiden.

Arriving at the island, Denver puts on a pippin of a costume, consisting of a deerstalker cap, a Prince Albert coat, and hip boots, and goes ashore to seek the girl he marooned. He has just vanished into the saw grass, declaiming away like Dion Boucicault, when the screen suddenly blacks out, or at least it did the day I saw the picture. I sprang up buoyantly, hoping that perhaps the film had caught fire and provided a solution for everybody's dilemma, but it had merely slipped off the sprocket. By the time it was readjusted, I, too, had slipped off, consumed a flagon or two, and was back in my chair waiting alertly for the payoff. I soon realized my blunder. I should have stayed in the rathskeller and had the projectionist phone it to me.

Denver becomes lost in the jungle very shortly, and when he fails to return to the yacht, two of the crew go in search of him. They meet Lieutenant Bond's scout, who has meanwhile made indecent overtures to the leopard girl and been declared a pariah by his fellows. The trio rescue Denver, but, for reasons that defy analysis, get plastered and plot to seize the yacht and sail away with the girl.

During all this katzenjammer, divers from the *Nautilus* have been reconnoitering around the craft to learn the identity of its owner, which presumably is emblazoned on its keel, inasmuch as one of them hastens to Nemo at top speed to announce with a flourish, "I have the honor to report that the yacht is owned by Charles Denver." The Captain forthwith stages a display of vindictive triumph that would have left Boris Thomashefsky, the great Yiddish tragedian, sick with envy; Denver, he apprises his companions, is the man against whom he has sworn undying vengeance. In the meantime (everything in *Twenty Thousand Leagues* happens in the meantime; the characters don't even sneeze consecutively), the villains kidnap the girl, are pursued to the yacht by Bond, and engage him in a fight to the death. At the psychological moment, a torpedo from the *Nautilus* blows up the whole shebang, extraneous characters are eliminated, and as the couple are hauled aboard the submarine, the big dramatic twist unfolds: Nemo is Prince Daaker and the girl his daughter. Any moviemaker with elementary decency would have recognized this as the saturation point and quit, but not the producer of *Twenty Thousand Leagues*. The picture bumbles on into a fantastically long-winded flashback of Nemo reviewing the whole Indian episode and relentlessly chewing the scenery to bits, and culminates with his demise and a strong suspicion in the onlooker that he has talked himself to death. His undersea burial, it must be admitted, has an authentic grisly charm. The efforts of the funeral party, clad in sober driving habit, to dig a grave in the ocean bed finally meet with defeat, and pettishly tossing the coffin into a clump of sea anemones, they stagger off.

GIRLFRIEND

An American GI who met Pablo Picasso in Paris told the artist that he didn't like modern paintings because they weren't realistic. Picasso made no immediate reply. A few minutes later the soldier showed him a snapshot of his girl friend.

"Carajo!" said Picasso, "Is she *really* as small as all that?"

The Dirty Nincompoop Who Edits That Journal

Frontier newspaper editors raised vituperation to a fine art - especially when lambasting one another. The following examples are from the Weekly Arizona Miner, *edited by John Marion at Prescott, and the* Arizona Sentinel, *edited by Judge William J. Berry at Yuma. The fact that the two men were old friends did not moderate the language.*

• • •

In the daily issue of (The Arizona *Miner*), this most scurrilous sheet of October 27th, we find an article in reference to ourself, which is altogether characteristic of the dirty nincompoop who edits that journal.

We shall not attempt to reply sciatim to the charge brought against us in said article, but will simply say that it is a batch of infernal falsehoods from beginning to end. The vile wretch who edits the *Miner* and who wrote that article, well knows, as every man in Arizona knows (who ever saw or heard him), that he is nothing if not a blackguard. He accuses us of being a gunsmith. We are proud of that, as many a man in Arizona will attest that we are a good one. Likewise we are a better editor and a better and more respectable man than he is which incontrovertible fact is well known. He charges us with demanding high prices for our gunsmith work. To that we say that we never got as much as our work was worth, and lost to the tune of fifteen hundred dollars by trusting certain treacherous scoundrels in Prescott and vicinity.

The miserable liar also says he let us write a communication for the *Miner*, years ago. Why, the shameless mongrel used to beg us to write for his foul abortion, and since we quit writing for it, many Arizonians say that the *Miner* is not worth a damn, and that is our opinion too, though we never expressed it publically before. Marion says we used to reside "up in Osegon!" Where is Osegon? (sic) We would like to know.

In regard to our being a "judge of whisky," we will simply say that no man ever saw Judge Wm. J. Berry laid out under its influence; while we had the extreme mortification of seeing the editor of the *Miner*, in a party given by Col. Baker in Prescott, laid out in the refreshment room, dead drunk, with candles placed at his head and feet, and a regular "wake" held over him.

As he lay, with drunken slobber issuing from his immense mouth, which extends from ear to ear, and his ears reaching up so high, everyone present was forcibly impressed with the fact that we had discovered the connecting link between the catfish and the jackass. What we have here faintly described is the truth, to attest which there are plenty of living witnesses. Now dry up, or we will come out with some more reminiscences.

(Arizona *Sentinel* of Nov. 7, 1874)

• • •

When two editors have such vivid personalities, each wants the last word. Since there is no pressing business at the time, a good fight adds sparkle to an infrequent moment of calm in the territory. Marion then replies to Berry's latest editorial with:

We had intended to let the mammoth ape whose name appears as editor of the Yuma *Sentinel* severely alone, until a day or two ago a citizen of Prescott requested us to inform our readers that Berry uttered a gratuitous falsehood when he stated that "he lost $1,500 by trusting certain treacherous scoundrels in Prescott and vicinity."

This being a reasonable and legitimate request, we now assert that Berry lied when he said so, and that it would take more than $1,500 to pay for the whisky which Berry "bummed" during his long sojourn in Prescott, not to speak of that which he guzzled in our sister city of Mohave, previous to the day upon which he found himself debarred from the privilege of swallowing whisky in Cerbat.

Again, we have been asked our reasons for not disputing certain assertions of his, regarding ourself. Well, one reason is: Berry is a natural and artificial liar, whom nobody was ever known to believe. Then, he did tell one truth about us, i.e., that drink once got the better of us. We were drunk that night, and have never yet attempted to deny it. But, Berry drank ten times to our once, and the only reason that he did not fall down and crawl on all fours like the cur that he is, was that there was not sufficient liquor in the house to fill his hogshead. Berry says no one ever saw him get drunk. When he lived in Prescott his first great care was to freight himself with whisky, after which it was his custom to walk like the swine that he is, on all fours, to his den.

He cannot have forgotten his visit to Lynx Creek, in 1864, when he rolled over a pine log, dead drunk, and served a useful purpose for a jacose man. Yes, Judge, we own up to that little drunk of ours; but unlike you, we were not pointed out and derided as a whisky bloat; nor did any person ever attempt to use us as a water-closet, as you were used that day on Lynx Creek.

As to your being a better editor than the writer of this, it is for the public to judge, not for you to assert, although you asserted it.

You have called us a blackguard, regardless of the old story about the kettle.

Then you have accused us of toadying to Gen. Cook; you, who have toadied and bent your knees to every placeholder, capitalist and bar-keeper in this section of Arizona; you, who made an egregious ass of yourself by firing an anvil salute in honor of Gen. Stoneman, who, you will recollect, never acknowledged the "honor done him." And you, who take up the cudgels for thieving Indian agents and, by doing so, go back on your record, made when you used to write and speak against the "Indian Ring Robbers and Murderers."

Ah, Judge, you have many masters; have been everything (except an independent man) by turns and nothing long. Had you changed shirts as often as you changed masters, there would be one sand-bar less in the Colorado River, and we would not know that you were in Yuma when, according to your published statement, you should be in San Francisco.

Hoping that these few lines will find you drunk and obedient to your masters, as usual, we say in our "classic" language, "uncork and be damned."

(Arizona Miner of Jan. 5, 1875)

THE STORY OF THE OLD RAM
by Mark Twain

Every now and then the boys used to tell me I ought to get one Jim Blaine to tell me the stirring story of his grandfather's old ram—but they always added that I must not mention the matter unless Jim was drunk at the time—just comfortably and sociably drunk. They kept this up until my curiosity was on the rack to hear the story. I got to haunting Blaine; but it was of no use, the boys always found fault with his condition; he was often moderately but never satisfactorily drunk. I never watched a man's condition with such absorbing interest; I never so pined to see a man uncompromisingly drunk before. At last, one evening I hurried to his cabin, for I learned that this time his situation was such that even the most fastidious could find no fault with it—he was tranquilly, serenely, symmetrically drunk—not a hiccup to mar his voice, not a cloud upon his brain thick enough to obscure his memory. As I entered, he was sitting upon an empty powder-keg, with a clay pipe in one hand and the other raised to command silence. His face was round, red, and very serious; his throat was bare and his hair tumbled; in general appearance and costume he was a stalwart miner of the period. On the pine table stood a candle, and its dim light revealed "the boys" sitting here and there on bunks, candle boxes, powder-kegs, etc. They said:

"Sh—! Don't speak—he's going to commence." I found a seat at once, and Blaine said:

"I don't reckon them times will ever come again. There never was a more bullier old ram than what he was. Grandfather fetched him from Illinois—got him of a man by the name of Yates—Bill Yates—maybe you might have heard of him; his father was a deacon—Baptist—and he was a rustler too; a man has to get up ruther early to get the start of old Thankful Yates; it was him that put the Greens up to joining teams with my grandfather when he moved west. Seth Green was prob'ly the pick of the flock; he married a Wilkerson—Sarah Wilkerson—good cretur, she was—one of the likeliest heifers that was ever raised in old Stoddard, everybody said that knowed her. She could heft a bar'l of flour as easy as I can flirt a flapjack. And spin? Don't mention it! Independent? Humph! When Sil Hawkins come a browsing around her, she let him know that for all his tin he couldn't trot in a harness alongside of her. You see, Sil Hawkins was—no, it warn't Sil Hawkins, after all—it was a galoot by the name of Filkins—I disremember his first name; but he was a stump—come into pra'r meeting drunk, one night, hooraying for Nixon, becuz he thought it was a primary; and old deacon Ferguson up and scooted him through the window and he lit on old Miss Jefferson's head, poor old filly. She was a good soul—had a glass eye and used to lend it to Old Miss Wagner, that hadn't any, to receive company in; it warn't big enough, and when Miss Wagner warn't noticing, it would get twisted around in the socket, and look up, maybe, or out to one side, and every which way, while t'other one was looking straight ahead as a spyglass. Grown people didn't mind it, but it most always made the children cry, it was sort of scary. She tried packing it in raw cotton, but it wouldn't work, somehow—the cotton would get loose and stick out and look so awful that the children couldn't stand it no way. She was always dropping it out, and turning up her old deadlight on the company empty, and making them uncomfortable, becuz she never could tell when it hopped out, being blind on that side, you see. So somebody would have to hunch her and say, "Your game eye has fetched loose, Miss Wagner dear"—and then all of them would have to sit and wait till she jammed it in again—wrong side before, as a general thing, and green as a bird's egg, being bashful cretur and easy sot back before company. But being wrong side before warn't much difference, anyway, becuz her own eye was sky-blue and the glass one was yaller on the front side, so whichever way she turned it didn't match nohow. Old Miss Wagner was considerable on the borrow, she was. When she had a quilting, or Dorcas S'iety at her house she gen'ally borrowed Miss Higgin's wooden leg to stump around on; it was considerable shorter than her other pin, but much she minded that. She said she couldn't abide crutches when she had company, becuz they were so slow; said when she had company and things had to be done, she wanted to get up and hump herself. She was as bald as a jug, and so she used to borrow Miss Jacops's wig—Miss Jacops was the coffin-peddler's wife—a ratty old buzzard, he was, that used to go roosting around where people was sick, waiting for 'em; and there that old rip would sit all day, in the shade, on a coffin that he judged would fit the can'idate; and if it was a slow customer and kind of uncertain, he'd fetch his rations and a blanket along and sleep in the coffin nights. He was anchored out that way, in frosty weather, for about three weeks, once, before old Robbins's place, waiting for him; and after that, for as much as two years, Jacops was not on speaking terms with the old man, on account of his disapp'inting him. He got one of his feet froze, and lost money, too, becuz old Robbins took a favorable turn and got well. The next time Robbins got sick, Jacops tried to make up with him, and varnished up the same old coffin and fetched it along; but old Robbins was too many for him, and 'peared to be powerful weak; he bought the coffin for ten dollars and Jacops was to pay it back and twenty-five more besides if Robbins didn't like the coffin after he'd tried it. And then Robbins dies, and at the funeral he bursted off the lid and riz up in his shroud and told the parson to let up on the performances, becuz he could not stand such a coffin as that. You see he had been in a trance once before, when he was young, and he took the chances on another, cal'lating that if he made the trip it was money in his pocket, and if he missed fire he couldn't lose a cent. And by George he sued Jacops for the rhino and got jedgment; and he set up the coffin in his back parlor and said he 'lowed to take his time, now. It was always an aggravation to Jacops, the way that miserable old thing acted. He moved back to Indiany pretty soon—went to Wellsville—Wellsville was the place the Hogadorns was from. Mighty fine family. Old Maryland stock. Old Squire Hogadorn could carry around more mixed licker, and cuss better than most any man I ever see. His second wife was the widder Billings—she that was Becky Martin; her dam was deacon Dunlap's first wife. Her oldest child, Maria, married a missionary and died in grace—et up by the savages. They et him, too, poor feller—biled him. It warn't the custom, so they say, but they explained to friends of his'n that went down there to bring away his things, that they'd tried missionaries every other way and never could get any good out of 'em—and so it annoyed all his relations to find out that man's life was fooled away just out of a dern'd experiment, so to speak. But mind you, there ain't anything ever really lost; everything that people can't understand and don't see the reason of does good if you only hold on and give it a fair shake; Prov'dence don't fire no blank ca'tridges, boys. That there missionary's substance, unbeknowns to himself, actu'ly converted every last one of them heathens that took a chance at the barbecue. Nothing ever fetched them but that. Don't tell me it was an accident that he was biled. There ain't no such thing as an accident. When my Uncle Lem was leaning up agin a scaffolding once, sick, drunk, or suthin, an Irishman with a hod full of bricks fell on him out of the third story and broke the old man's back in two places. People said it was an accident. Much accident there was about that. He didn't know what he was there for, but he was there for a good object. If he hadn't been there the Irishman would've been killed. Nobody can ever make me believe anything different from that. Uncle Lem's dog was there. Why didn't the Irishman fall on the dog? Becuz the dog would a seen him a coming and stood from under. That's the reason the dog warn't appinted. A dog can't be depended on to carry out a special providence. Mark my words it was a put-up thing. Accidents don't happen, boys. Uncle Lem's dog—I wish you could a seen that dog. He was a reglar shepherd—or ruther he was part bull and part shepherd—splendid animal; belonged to the Western Reserve Hagars; prime family; his mother was a Watson; one of his sisters married a Wheeler; they settled in Morgan County, and he got nipped by the machinery in a carpet factory and went through in less than a quarter of a minute; his widder bought the piece of carpet that had his remains wove in, and people come a hundred mile to 'tend the funeral. There was fourteen yards in the piece. She wouldn't let them roll him up, but planted him just so—full length. The church was middling small where they preached the funeral, and they had to let him stand up, same as a monument. And they nailed a sign on it and put—put on—put on it—Sacred to the M-e-m-o-r-y—of fourteen—y-a-r-d-s-of three-ply-car . . . pet—containing all that was m-o-r-t-a-l-of-of-W-i-l-l-i-a-m-W-h-e—"

Jim Blaine had been growing gradually drowsy and drowsier—his head nodded, once, twice, three times—dropped peacefully upon his breast, and he fell tranquilly asleep. The tears were running down the boys' cheeks—they had been from the start, though I had never noticed it. I perceived that I was "sold." I learned then that Jim Blaine's peculiarity was that whenever he reached a certain stage of intoxication, no human power could keep him from setting out, with impressive unction, to tell about a wonderful adventure which he had once had with his Grandfather's old ram—and the mention of the ram in the first sentence was as far as any man had ever heard him get, concerning it. He always maundered off, interminably, from one thing to another, till his whiskey got the better of him and he fell asleep. What the thing was that happened to him and his grandfather's old ram is a dark mystery to this day, for nobody has ever yet found out.

–from *Roughing It*

Lectures on Astronomy
by John Phoenix

The following pages were originally prepared in the form of a course of lectures to be delivered before the Lowell Institute, of Boston, Mass., but, owing to the unexpected circumstance of the author's receiving no invitation to lecture before that institution, they were laid aside shortly after their completion.

Under these circumstances, and yielding with reluctance to the earnest solicitations of many eminent scientific friends, the author has been induced to place the Lectures before the public in their present form; it being his greatest ambition to render himself useful in his day and generation, by widely disseminating the information he has acquired among those who, less fortunate, are yet willing to receive instruction.

San Diego Observatory, September 1, 1854

(Following a thoroughly ludicrous examination per the history of astronomy, Phoenix takes up the particulars.)

As in this world you will hardly ever find a man so small but that he has someone else smaller than he to look up to and revolve around him, so in the Solar System we find that the majority of the planets have one or more smaller planets revolving around them. These small bodies are termed secondaries, moons or satellites—the planets themselves being called primaries.

We know at present of eighteen primaries; viz., Mercury, Venus, the Earth, Mars, Flora, Vesta, Iris, Metis, Hebe, Astrea, Juno, Ceres, Pallas, Hygeia, Jupiter, Saturn, Herschel, Neptune, and another unnamed. There are distributed among these, nineteen secondaries, all of which, except our Moon, are invisible to the naked eye.

We shall now proceed to consider, separately, the different bodies composing the Solar System, and to make known what little information, comparatively speaking, science has collected regarding them. And first in order, as in place, we come to:

The Sun

This glorious orb may be seen almost any clear day, by looking intently in its direction through a piece of smoked glass. Through this medium it appears about the size of a large orange, and of much the same color. It is, however, somewhat larger, being, in fact, 887,000 miles in diameter, and containing a volume of matter equal to fourteen-hundred thousand globes of the size of the Earth. Through the telescope it appears like an enormous globe of fire, with many spots upon its surface, which, unlike those of the leopard, are continually changing. These spots were first discovered by a gentleman named Galileo, in the year 1611. Though the Sun is usually termed and considered the luminary of day, it may not be uninteresting to our readers to know that it certainly has been seen in the night. A scientific friend of ours from New England (Mr. R. W. Emerson), while traveling through the northern part of Norway, with a cargo of tinware, on the 21st of June, 1836, distinctly saw the Sun in all its majesty, shining at midnight!—in fact, shining all night! Emerson is not what you would call a superstitious man, by any means—but he left! Since that time many persons have observed its nocturnal appearance in that part of the country, at the same time of the year. This phenomenon has never been witnessed in the latitude of San Diego, however, and it is very improbable that it ever will be. Sacred history informs us that a distinguished military man named Joshua once caused the Sun to "stand still;" how he did it is not mentioned. There can, of course, be no doubt of the fact that he arrested its progress, and possibly caused it to "stand *still*"—but translators are not always perfectly accurate, and we are inclined to the opinion that it might have wiggled a very little, when Joshua was not looking directly at it. The statement, however, does not appear so very incredible, when we reflect that seafaring men are in the habit of actually bringing the Sun *down to the horizon* every day at 12 Meridian. This they effect by means of a tool made of brass, glass and silver, called a sextant.

The composition of the Sun has long been a matter of dispute. By close and accurate observation with an excellent opera-glass, we have arrived at the conclusion that its entire surface is covered with water to a great depth; which water, being composed by a process known at the present only to the Creator of the Universe and Mr. Paine, of Worcester, Massachusetts, generates carbureted hydrogen gas, which, being inflamed, surrounds the entire body with an ocean of fire, from which we and the other planets receive our light and heat. The spots upon its surface are glimpses of water obtained through the fire; and we call the attention of our old friend and former schoolmate, Mr. Agassiz, to this fact; as by closely observing one of these spots with a strong refracting telescope, he may discover a new species of fish, with little fishes inside of them. It is possible that the Sun may burn out after awhile, which would leave this world in a state of darkness quite uncomfortable to contemplate; but even under these circumstances it is pleasant to reflect that courting and love-making would probably increase to an indefinite extent, and that many persons would make large fortunes by the sudden rise in value of coal, wood, candles, and gas, which would go to illustrate the truth of the old proverb, "It's an ill wind that blows nobody any good."

Upon the whole, the Sun is a glorious creation; pleasing to gaze upon (through smoked glass), elevating to think upon, and exceedingly comfortable to every created being on a cold day; it is the largest, the brightest, and may be considered by far the most magnificent object in the celestial sphere; though with all these attributes it must be confessed that it is occasionally entirely eclipsed by the moon.

Mercury

This planet, with the exception of the asteroids, is the smallest of the system. It is the nearest to the Sun, and, in consequence, cannot be seen (on account of the Sun's superior light) except at its greatest eastern and western elongations, which occur in March and April, August and September, when it may be seen for a short time immediately after sunset and shortly before sunrise. It then appears like a star of the first magnitude, having a white twinkling light, and resembling somewhat the star Regulus in the constellation Leo. The day in Mercury is about ten minutes longer than ours, its year is about equal to three of our months. It receives six and a half times as much heat from the Sun as we do; from which we conclude that the climate must be very similar to that of Fort Yuma, on the Colorado River. The difficulty of communication with Mercury will probably prevent its ever being selected as a military post; though it possesses many advantages for that purpose, being extremely inaccessible, inconvenient, and, doubtless, singularly uncomfortable. It receives its name from the God,

Mercury, in the Heathen Mythology, who is the patron and tutelary Divinity of San Diego County.

Venus

This beautiful planet may be seen either a little after sunset, or shortly before sunrise, accordingly as it becomes the morning or evening star, but never departing quite 48° from the Sun. Its day is about twenty-five minutes shorter than ours; its year seven and a half months, or thirty-two weeks. The diameter of Venus is 7,700 miles, and she receives from the Sun thrice as much light and heat as the Earth.

An old Dutchman named Schroeter spent more than ten years in observations on this planet, and finally discovered a mountain on it twenty-two miles in height, but he never could discover any thing on the mountain, not even a mouse, and finally died about as wise as when he commenced his studies.

Venus, in Mythology, was a Goddess of singular beauty, who became the wife of Vulcan, the blacksmith, and, we regret to add, behaved in the most immoral manner after her marriage. The celebrated case of Vulcan vs. Mars, and the consequent scandal, is probably still fresh in the minds of our readers. By a large portion of society, however, she was considered an ill-used and persecuted lady, against whose high tone of morals and strictly virtuous conduct not a shadow of suspicion could be cast; Vulcan, by the same parties, was considered a horrid brute, and they all agreed that it served him right when he lost his case and had to pay the court costs. Venus still remains the Goddess of Beauty, and not a few of her protégés may be found in California.

The Earth

The Earth, or as the Latins called it, Tellus (from which originated the expression, "do tell us"), is the third planet in the Solar System, and the one on which we subsist, with all our important joys and sorrows. The San Diego Herald is published weekly on this planet, for five dollars per annum, payable invariably in advance. As the Earth is by no means the most important planet in the system, there is no reason to suppose that it is particularly distinguished from the others by being inhabited. It is reasonable, therefore, to conclude that all the other planets of the system are filled with living, moving and sentient beings; and as some of them are superior to Earth in size and position, it is not improbable that their inhabitants may be superior to us in physical and mental organization.

But if this were a demonstrable fact, instead of a mere hypothesis, it would be found a very difficult matter to persuade us of its truth. To the inhabitants of Venus, the Earth appears like a brilliant star, very much, in fact, as Venus appears to us; and, reasoning from analogy, we are led to believe that the election of Mr. Pierce, the European war, or the split in the great Democratic party produced but very little excitement among them.

To the inhabitants of Jupiter, our important globe appears like a small star of the fourth or fifth magnitude. We recollect some years ago gazing with astonishment upon the inhabitants of a drop of water, developed by the Solar Microscope, and secretly wondering whether they were or not reasoning beings, with souls to be saved. It is not altogether a pleasant reflection that a highly scientific inhabitant of Jupiter, armed with a telescope of (to us) inconceivable form, may be pursuing a similar course of inquiry, and indulging in similar speculations regarding our Earth and its inhabitants. Gazing with a curious eye, his attention is suddenly attracted by the movements of a grand celebration of Fourth of July in New York, or a mighty convention in Baltimore. "God bless my soul!" he exclaims; "I declare, they're alive, these little creatures; do see them wriggle!" To an inhabitant of the Sun, however, he of Jupiter is probably quite as insignificant, and the Sun man is possibly a mere atom in the opinion of a dweller in Sirius. A little reflection on these subjects leads to the opinion that the death of an individual man on this Earth, though perhaps as important an event as can occur to himself, is calculated to cause no great convulsion of Nature, or disturb particularly the great aggregate of created beings.

The earth moves around the sun from west to east in a year, and turns on its axis in a day; thus moving at the rate of 68,000 miles an hour in its orbit, and rolling around at the tolerably rapid rate of 1,040 miles per hour. As our readers may have seen, when a man is galloping a horse violently over a smooth road, if the horse, from viciousness or other cause, suddenly stops, the man keeps on at the same rate over the animal's head; so we, supposing the Earth to be suddenly arrested on its axis—men, women, children, horses, cattle and sheep, donkeys, editors and members of Congress, with all our goods and chattels—would be thrown off into the air at the speed of 173 miles a minute, every mother's son of us describing the arc of a parabola, which is probably the only description we should ever be able to give of the affair.

The catastrophe, to one sufficiently collected to enjoy it, would doubtless be exceedingly amusing; but as there would probably be no time for laughing, we pray that it may not occur until after our demise; when, should it take place, our monument will probably accompany the movement.

It is a singular fact, that if a man travels 'round the Earth in an eastwardly direction, he will find, on returning to the place of departure, he has gained one whole day; the reverse of this proposition being true also, it follows that the Yankees, who are constantly traveling to the West, do not live as long by a day or two as they would if they had stayed home; and supposing each Yankee's time to be worth $1.50 per day, it may be easily shown that a considerable amount of money is annually lost by their roving dispositions.

Science is yet but in its infancy; with its growth, new discoveries of an astounding nature will doubtless be made, among which, probably, will be some method by which the course of the Earth may be altered, and it be steered with the same ease and regularity through space and among the stars as a steamboat is now directed through water. It will be a very interesting spectacle to see the Earth "rounding to," with her head to the air, off Jupiter, while the moon is sent off laden with mails and passengers for that planet, to bring back the return mails and a large party of rowdy Jupiterians going to attend a grand prize fight in the ring of Saturn.

Well, Christopher Columbus would have been just as much astonished at a revelation of the steamboat and the locomotive engine as we should be to witness the above performance, which our intelligent posterity during the ensuing year, A.D. 2,000, will possibly look upon as a very ordinary and commonplace affair.

Only three days ago we asked a medium where Sir John Franklin was at that time; to which he replied he was cruising about (officers and crew all well) on the interior of the Earth, to which he had obtained entrance through Symmes Hole!

With a few remarks upon the Earth's satellite, we conclude the first Lecture on Astronomy; the remainder of the course being contained in a second Lecture, treating the planets Mars, Jupiter, Saturn and Neptune, the Asteroids, and the fixed stars, which last, being "fixings," are, according to Mr. Charles Dickens, American property.

The Moon

This resplendent luminary, like a youth on the 4th of July, has its first quarter; like a ruined spendthrift, its last quarter; and, like an omnibus, is occasionally full and new. The evenings on which it appears between these last stages are beautifully illumined by its clear, mellow light.

The Moon revolves in an elliptical orbit about the Earth in twenty-nine days, twelve hours, forty-four minutes and three seconds—the time which elapses between one new Moon and another. It was supposed by the ancient philosophers that the Moon was made of green cheese, an opinion still entertained by the credulous and ignorant. Kepler and Tycho Brahe, however, held to the opinion that it was composed of Charlotte Russe, the dark portions of its surface being sponge cake, the light *blanc mange*. Modern advances in science, and the use of Lord Rosse's famous telescope, have demonstrated the absurdity of all these speculations by proving conclusively that the Moon is mainly composed of the *Ferrosesqui-cyanuret*, of the *cyanide of potassium!*

Up to the latest dates from the Atlantic States, no one has succeeded in reaching the Moon. Should any one do so hereafter, it will probably be a woman, as the sex will never cease making exertion for that purpose as long as there is a man in it.

Upon the whole, we may consider the Moon an excellent institution, among the many we enjoy under a free, republican form of government, and it is a blessed thing to reflect that the President of the United States cannot veto it, no matter how strong an inclination he may feel, from principle or habit, to do so.

It has been ascertained beyond a doubt that the Moon has no air. Consequently, the common expressions, "The Moon was gazing down with an air of benevolence," or with "an air of complacency," or with "an air of calm superiority," are incorrect and objectionable, the fact being that the moon has no air at all.

The existence of the celebrated "Man in the Moon" has been frequently questioned by modern philosophers. The whole subject is involved in doubt and obscurity. The only authority we have for believing that such an individual exists, and has been seen and spoken with, is a fragment of an old poem composed by an ancient

Astronomer by the name of Goose, which has been handed down to us as follows:

> *"The man in the Moon, came down too soon*
> *To inquire the way to Norwich;*
> *The man in the South, he burned his mouth,*
> *Eating cold, hot porridge."*

The evidence conveyed in this distich is, however, rejected by the skeptical among the modern Astronomers, who consider the passage an allegory—"The man in the South" being supposed typical of the late John C. Calhoun, and the "cold, hot porridge" alluding to the project of nullification.

IBM Sent This?

This is an actual alert to IBM field engineers and went out to all IBM branch offices.

Mouse balls are now available as field replacement units. Therefore, if a mouse fails to operate or should it perform erratically, it may need a ball replacement. Because of the delicate nature of this procedure, replacement of mouse balls should only be attempted by trained personnel.

Before proceeding, determine the type of mouse ball by examining the underside of the mouse. Domestic balls will be larger and harder than foreign balls. Ball removal procedures differ depending upon the manufacturer of the mouse. Foreign balls can be replaced using the pop-off method. Domestic balls can be replaced using the twist-off method. Mouse balls are not usually static sensitive. However, excessive handling can result in sudden discharge. Upon completion of ball replacement, the mouse may be used immediately.

It is recommended that each replacer have a pair of spare balls for maintaining optimum customer satisfaction and that any cutstomer missing his balls should suspect local personnel of removing these items.

THE LATEST IMPROVEMENTS IN ARTILLERY
by Orpheus C. Kerr
(Robert H. Newell)

By invitation of a well-known official, I visited the Navy-yard yesterday and witnessed the trial of some newly-invented rifled cannon. The trial was of short duration, and the jury brought in a verdict of "innocent of any intent to kill."

The first gun tried was similar to those used in the Revolution, except that it had a larger touch-hole, and the carriage was painted green instead of blue. This novel and ingenious weapon was pointed at a target about sixty yards distant. It didn't hit it, and as nobody saw any ball, there was much perplexity expressed. A midshipman did say that he thought the ball must have run out of the touch-hole when they loaded up—for which he was instantly expelled from the service. After a long search without finding the ball, there was some thought of summoning the Naval Retiring Board to decide on the matter, when somebody happened to look into the mouth of the cannon and discovered that the ball hadn't gone out at all. The inventor said this would happen sometimes, especially if you didn't put a brick over the touch-hole when you fired the gun. The Government was so pleased with this explanation that it ordered forty of the guns on the spot, at six hundred thousand dollars apiece, the guns to be furnished as soon as the war was over.

The next weapon tried was Jink's double back-action revolving cannon for ferryboats. It consists of a heavy bronze tube, revolving on a pivot, with both ends open, and a touch-hole in the middle. While one gunner puts a load in at one end, another puts in a load at the other end, and one touch-hole serves for both. Upon applying the match, the gun is whirled swiftly round on a pivot, and both balls fly out in circles, causing great slaughter on both sides. This terrible engine was aimed at the target with great accuracy; but as the gunner has a large family dependent on him for support, he refused to apply the match. The Government was satisfied without firing and ordered six of the guns at a million dollars apiece, the guns to be furnished in time for our next war.

The last weapon subjected to trial was a mountain howitzer of a new pattern. The inventor explained that its great advantage was that it required no powder. In battle it is placed on the top of a high mountain, and a ball slipped loosely into it. As the enemy passes the foot of the mountain, the gunner in charge tips over the howitzer, and the ball rolls down the side of the mountain into the midst of the doomed foe. The range of this terrible weapon depends greatly on the height of the mountain and the distance to its base. The Government ordered forty of these mountain howitzers at a hundred thousand dollars apiece, to be planted on the first mountains discovered in the enemy's country.

There is much sensation in nautical circles arising from the immoral conduct of the rebel privateers; but public feeling has been somewhat easier since the invention of a craft for capturing the pirates, by an ingenious Connecticut chap. Yesterday he exhibited a small model of it at a cabinet meeting, and explained it thus:

"You will perceive," says he to the President, "that the machine itself will only be four times the size of the *Great Eastern*, and need not cost over a few billion dollars. I have only got to discover one thing before I can make it perfect. You will observe that it has a steam-engine on board. This engine works a pair of immense iron clamps, which are let down into the water from the extreme end of a very lengthy horizontal spar. Upon approaching the pirate, the captain orders the engineer to put on steam. Instantly the clamps descend from the end of the spar and clutch the privateer athwartships. Then the engine is reversed, the privateer is lifted bodily out of the water, the spar swings around over the deck, and the pirate ship is let down into the hold by the run. Then shut your hatches, and you have ship and pirates safe and sound."

The President's gothic features lighted up beautifully at the words of the great inventor; but in a moment they assumed an expression of doubt, and says he:

"But how are you going to manage, if the privateer fires upon you while you are doing this?"

"My dear sir," says the inventor, "I told you I had only one thing to discover before I could make the machine perfect, and that's it."

—*1861*

BEAUTIFUL GIRL

The following correspondence comes from a popular woman's magazine of the 1950s.

Oct. 4, 1956

I am an unmarried woman, very glamorous looking and I have an irresistible personality yet I haven't a man. Why? I look around and most of the married women I see are positively ugly. Is there something wrong with men, or should I de-glamorize myself?

—*Beautiful Girl*

Her sympathetic respondents:

No, honey. Don't de-glamorize yourself. Just plug up that hole in your head.

—*Mrs. V.M.*

Tell that baffled beauty to look in her mirror again. Even a monkey thinks he's beautiful.

—*Another Woman*

Third World Driving
by P.J. O'Rourke

During the past couple years I've had to do my share of driving in the Third World—in Mexico, Lebanon, the Philippines, Cyprus, El Salvador, Africa and Italy. (Italy is not technically part of the Third World, but no one has told the Italians.) I don't pretend to be an expert, but I have been making notes. Perhaps these notes will be useful to readers who are planning to do something really stupid with their Hertz #1 Club cards.

Road Hazards

What would be a road hazard anyplace else, in the Third World is probably the road. There are two techniques for coping with this. One is to drive very fast so your wheels "get on top" of the ruts and your car sails over the ditches and gullies. Predictably, this will result in disaster. The other technique is to drive very slow. This will also result in disaster. No matter how slowly you drive into a ten-foot hole, you're still going to get hurt. You'll find the locals themselves can't make up their minds. Either they drive at 2 mph—which they do every time there's absolutely no way to get around them. Or else they drive at 100 mph—which they do coming right at you when you finally get a chance to pass the guy going 2 mph.

Basic Information

It's important to have your facts straight before piloting a car around an underdeveloped county. For instance, which side of the road do they drive on? This is easy. They drive on your side. That is, you can depend on it, any oncoming traffic will be on your side of the road. Also, how do you translate kilometers into miles? Most people don't know this, but one kilometer equals ten miles, exactly. True, a kilometer is only 62 percent of a mile, but, if something is one hundred kilometers away, read that as one thousand miles because the roads are 620 percent worse than anything you've ever seen. And when you see a 50-kph speed limit, you might as well figure that means 500 mph because nobody cares. The Third World does not have Broderick Crawford and the Highway Patrol. Outside the cities, it doesn't have many police at all. Law enforcement is in the hands of the army. And soldiers, if they feel like it, will shoot you no matter what speed you are going.

Traffic Signs and Signals

Most developing nations use international traffic symbols. Americans may find themselves perplexed by road signs that look like Boy Scout merit badges and by such things as an iguana silhouette with a red diagonal bar across it. Don't worry, the natives don't know what they mean either. The natives do, however, have an elaborate set of signals used to convey information to the traffic around them. For example, if you're trying to pass someone and he blinks his left turn signal, it means go ahead. Either that or it means a large truck is coming around the bend, and you'll get killed if you try. You'll find out in a moment.

Signaling is further complicated by festive decorations found on many vehicles. It can be hard to tell a hazard flasher from a string of Christmas-tree lights wrapped around the bumper, and brake lights can easily be confused with the dozen red Jesus statuettes and the ten stuffed animals with blinking eyes on the package shelf.

Dangerous Curves

Dangerous curves are marked, at least in Christian lands, by white wooden crosses positioned to make the curves even more dangerous. These crosses are memorials to people who've died in traffic accidents, and they give a rough statistical indication of how much trouble you're likely to have at that spot in the road. Thus, when you come through a curve in a full-power slide and are suddenly confronted with a veritable forest of crucifixes, you know you're dead.

Learning To Drive Like A Native

It's important to understand that in the Third World most driving is done with the horn, or the "Egyptian Brake Pedal," as it is known. There is a precise and complicated etiquette of horn use. Honk your horn only under the following circumstances:

1. When anything blocks the road.
2. When anything doesn't.

3. When anything might.
4. At red lights.
5. At green lights.
6. At all other times.

Road Blocks

One thing you can count on in Third World countries is trouble. There's always some uprising, coup or Marxist insurrection going on, and this means military roadblocks. There are two kinds of military roadblocks: the kind where you slow down so they can look you over, and the kind where you come to a full stop so they can steal your luggage. The important thing is that you must *never* stop at the slow-down kind of roadblock. If you stop, they'll think you're a terrorist about to attack them, and they'll shoot you. And you must *always* stop at the full-stop kind of roadblock. If you just slow down, they'll think you're a terrorist about to attack them, and they'll shoot you. How do you tell the difference between the two kinds of roadblocks? You can't.

(The terrorists, of course, have roadblocks of their own. They always make you stop. Sometimes with land mines.)

Animals In The Right Of Way

As a rule, slow down for donkeys, speed up for goats and stop for cows. Donkeys will get out of your way eventually, and so will pedestrians. But never actually stop for either of them or they'll take advantage, especially the pedestrians. If you stop in the middle of a crowd of Third World pedestrians, you'll be there buying Chiclets and bogus antiquities for days.

Drive like hell through the goats. It's almost impossible to hit a goat. On the other hand, it's almost impossible *not* to hit a cow. Cows are immune to horn-honking, shouting, swats with sticks and taps on the hind quarters with the bumper. The only thing you can do to make a cow move is swerve to avoid it, which will make the cow move in front of you with lightening speed.

The most dangerous animals are the chickens. In the United States, when you see a ball roll into the street, you hit your brakes because you know the next thing you'll see is a kid chasing it. In the Third World, it's not balls the kids are chasing, but chickens. Are they practicing punt returns with a leghorn? Dribbling it? Playing stick-hen? I don't know. But Third Worlders are remarkably fond of their chickens and, also, their children (population problems not withstanding). If you hit one or both, they may survive. But you will not.

Accidents

Never look where you're going—you'll only scare yourself. Nonetheless, try to avoid collisions. There are bound to be more people in that bus, truck or even on that Moped than there are in your car. At best you'll be screamed deaf. And if the police do happen to be around, standard procedure is to throw everyone in jail regardless of fault. This is done to forestall blood feuds, which are a popular hobby in many of these places. Remember the American consul is very busy fretting about that Marxist insurrection, and it may be months before he comes to visit.

If you have an accident, the only thing to do is go on the offensive. Throw big wads of American money at everyone, and hope for the best.

Safety Tips

One nice thing about the Third World, you don't have to fasten your safety belt (or stop smoking, or cut down on saturated fats). It takes a lot off your mind when average life expectancy is forty-five minutes.

HE QUIT SNORING

" . . . and damned if Clem Chickasaw weren't killed last week, sleeping off a drunk at Grass Range. Seems Clem had a little more rye on board than usual, but not enough to suite him. So the sumbitch goes and takes a booze joint. After smoking up the place and running everybody out he helps himself to the hooch and falls asleep. Folks said they could hear him snoring all the way out on the Honeyquim spread. Well, the booze boss gets a gun and comes back and catches Clem slumberin'. Old Clem never woke up, but he quit snoring."

—*from a letter by Judge Roy "Tall" Cotten to his brother*
Amarillo, Texas, 1873

Jud Brownin Hears Ruby Play

by George W. Bagby

"Jud, they say you heard Rubenstein play when you were in New York?"

"I did, for a fact."

"Well, tell us all about it."

"What! Me? I might's well tell you about the creation of the world."

"Come, now. Go ahead."

"Well, sir, he had the blamedest, biggest, catty-corneredest pianner you ever laid your eyes on—something like a distracted billiard table on three legs. The lid was heisted, and mighty well it was. If it hadn't, he'd a-tore the entire sides clean out and scattered 'em to the four winds of heaven.

"*Played well?* You bet he did. When he first sit down, he 'peered to care mighty little about playing, and wished he hadn't come. He tweedle-eedled a little on the treble, and twoodle-oodled some on the bass—just fooling and boxing the thing's jaws for being in his way.

"I says to a man setting next to me, says I, 'What sort of fool playing is that?' And he says, 'Hesh!' But presently Ruby's hands commenced chasing one another up and down the keys, like a passel of rats scampering through a garret very swift. Parts of it was sweet, though, and reminded me of a sugar squirrel turning the wheel of a candy cage.

" 'Now,' says I to my neighbor, 'he's showing off. He ain't got no idea, no plan of nothing. If he'd play me a tune of some kind or other I'd-'

"But my neighbor says, 'Hesh!' very impatient.

"I was jist about to give up and go home, being tired of that foolishness, when I heard a little bird waking up away off in the woods, and calling sleepy-like, and I looked up and see Ruby was beginning to take some interst in his business, and I sit down again.

"It was the peep of day. The light come faint from the east, the breezes blowed fresh, some more birds waked up in the orchard, then some more in the trees near the house and the gal opened the shutters. Just then the first beam of the sun fell on the garden and it teched the roses on the bushes, and the next thing it was broad day. The sun fairly blazed. The birds sung like they'd split their throats. All the leaves was moving and flashing diamonds of dew and the whole world was bright and happy as a king. Seemed to me like there was a good breakfast in every house in the land, and not a sick child or woman anywhere. It was a fine morning.

"And I says to my neighbor, 'That's fine music, that is.'

"But he glared at me like he'd like to cut my throat.

"By and by, the wind turned. It began to thicken up, and a kind of gray mist come over things. I got low-spirited directly. Then a silver rain begun to fall. I could see the drops touch the ground, and flash up and roll away. I could smell the wet flowers in the meadow, but the sun didn't shine, nor the birds sing, and it was a foggy day, pretty but kind of melancholy.

"Then the moonlight come, without any sunset, and shone on the graveyards, where some few ghosts lifted their hands and went over the wall. And between the black, sharp-top trees, there was fine houses with ladies in the lit-up windows, and men that loved 'em, but could never git a-nigh 'em, who played on gittars under the trees, and made me so miserable I could a-cried, because I wanted to love somebody, I don't know who, better than the men with gittars did.

"Then the moon went down, it got dark, the wind moaned and wept like a lost child for its dead mother, and I could a-got up then and there and preached a better sermon than John Calvin. There wasn't a thing left in the world to live for, not a blame thing, and yet I didn't want the music to stop one bit. It was happier to be miserable. I hung my head and pulled out my handkerchief, and blowed my nose to keep from crying. My eyes is weak, anyway, and I didn't want anybody to be a-gazing at me a-sniveling. It's nobody's business what I do with my nose. It's mine. But some several glared at me mad as Tucker.

"And all of a sudden, old Ruby changed his tune. He ripped out and he rared, he tipped and he tared, he pranced and he charged like the grand entry at a circus. Peared to me that all the gaslights in the house was turned on at once, things got so bright, and I hilt up my head, ready to look any man in the face, and not afraid of nothing. It was a circus, and a brass band, and a big ball,

all going on at the same time. He lit into them keys like a thousand ton of brick. He gave 'em no rest, day or night. He set every living joint in me a-going, and not being able to stand it no longer, I jumped spang onto my seat, and jest hollered—

" 'Go for it, my Rube!'

"Every blamed man, woman and child in the house riz on me, and shouted, 'Put him out, put him out!'

" 'Put your great-grandmother's grizzly gray cat into the middle of next month!' I says. 'Tech me if you dare. I paid my money, and you jest come a-nigh me!'

"With that, some several policeman run up, and I had to simmer down. But I would a-fit any fool that laid hands on me, for I was bound to hear Ruby out or die.

"He had changed his tune again. He hop-light ladies and tip-toed fine from end to end of the keyboard. He played soft and low and solemn. I heard the church bells over the hills. I saw the stars rise—then the music changed to water, full of feeling that couldn't be thought, and begun to drop-drip, drop-drip, drop, clear and sweet, falling into a lake of glory. It was too sweet. I tell you the audience cheered. Rubin, he kind of bowed, like he wanted to say, 'Much obliged, but I'd rather you wouldn't interrupt me.'

"He stopped a moment or two to ketch breath. Then he got mad. He run his fingers through his hair, he shoved up his sleeve, he opened his coat tails a little further, he drug up his stool, he leaned over, and, sir, he jest went for that old pianner. He slapped her face, he boxed her jaws, he pulled her nose, he pinched her ears, and he scratched her cheeks until she fairly yelled. She bellered like a bull, she bleated like a calf, she howled like a hound, she squealed like a pig, she shrieked like a rat, and *then* he would not let her up. He run a quarter stretch down the low grounds of the bass, till he got clean in the bowels of the earth, and you heard thunder galloping after thunder, through the hollows and caves of perdition. Then he foxed-chased his right hand with his left till he got way out of the treble into the clouds, where the notes was finer than the points of cambric needles, and you couldn't hear nothing bit the shadders of 'em.

"And *then* he wouldn't let the old pianner go. He forward two'd, he crossed over first gentleman, he sashayed right and left, back to your places, he all hands'd round, ladies to the right, promenade all, here and there, back and forth, up and down, perpetual motion, double twisted and turned and tacked and tangled into forty-eleven thousand double bow knots.

"By jinks, it was a mixtery! He fetched up his right wing, he fetched up his left wing, he fetched up his center, he fetched up his reserves. He fired by file, by platoons, companies, regiments, brigades. He opened his cannon-round shot, shells, shrapnels, grape, canister, mines and magazines-every living battery and bomb a-going at the same time. The house trembled, the lights danced, the walls shuck, the sky split, the ground rocked-heavens and earth, creation, sweet potatoes, Moses, ninepences, glory, ten penny nails, Sampson in a 'simmon tree—Bang!!! lang! perlang! P-r-r-r-r!! Bang!!!

"With that bang! he lifted himself bodily into the air, and he come down with his knees, fingers, toes, elbows, and his nose, striking every single solitary key on the pianner at the same time.

"The thing busted and went off into fifty-seven thousand five hundred and forty-two hemi-demi-semi quivers, and I knowed no more that evening."

Budding Actor

"Dad, guess what? I've got my first part in a play," said the budding young actor. "I play the part of a man who has been married for 25 years."

"That's a good start, son," replied the father. "Just keep at it and one of these days you'll get a speaking part."

King Kong Comes to Wabag
by John Long

D.B. looked confused as he pointed to a blurb headlined, "Two Die in Enga Fight." I grabbed the newspaper and skimmed the story: "Two men died of ax and arrow wounds on Friday after a fight broke out between Lyonai and Kundu outside of Wabag, in Enga Province. Joseph Yalya, thirty-eight, of Pina Village, died of an ax wound to the neck and Tumai Tupige, thirty-nine, also of Pina Village, died from an arrow through the chest. Police said about 800 men were involved in the fight. The fight broke out when Lyonai tribesmen accused the Kundu clan of using sorcery to kill a Lyonai elder."

Two casualties seemed rather modest for an 800-man brawl, but this was Papua, New Guinea, which some say God made first, when his technique was a little raw. Since every production resembles its creator, it follows that God is both insane and a genius, for everyone, natives included, stumble around Papua in a sort of daze, half astonished, half bored. D.B. and I had gone there strictly for the hell of it, looking for novelty, and were presently licking wounds after a nine-week exploratory thrash down the Strickland Gorge. We'd had a rough go of it, but after two days kicking around Mt. Hagan in the remote Highlands, we were jumpy for another epic. Our flight to Sydney and then to California was leaving in eight days, so it would have to be a quick one. Fact was, we'd worked and scrimped to fly to the far side of the globe, had hacked down that hateful gully all those weeks to stumble out the ass end with little more than dysentery. But one look at that newspaper article and our prospects brightened.

We snagged a ride from Solomon Chang, a crazy, high-strung engineer of Chinese/Papuan parentage. Chang was driving to a reservoir project at road's end, twenty-odd miles past Wabag, and wasn't expected there till the following day. The road, known as the "Highland Direct," was straighter than the Oregon coastline, but rockier; and this gave Chang nearly five hours to ramble on about native "warfare."

"The buggers spill onto the road sometimes," Chang said, "but they'll usually stop for cars. Maybe bum a smoke or two. And I've never seen them fight through lunch neither."

So there was more than a few histrionics to this warfare, though according to Chang somebody eventually had to die "to preserve the honor of the contest."

We had a solid week to get into trouble. Chang only had that night, but liked his chances. However, when we wheeled into that verdant toilet known as Wabag, we were disappointed not to have to continuously duck a salvo of spears and arrows. Rather, the same old routine: Kanakas dressed only in "ass-grass" (a thatch of kunai grass in front and back, secured with a leather belt), with axes over their shoulders, feathers or boar tusks through their septums, and as always, every jowl bulging of betel nut and rancorous red spit. We were right back to swatting mosquitos again. But our boredom was nothing compared to Chang's.

"Look," Chang said. "We ferret out some chief, thrash his ass and make off with his daughters." He considered for a moment. "Better yet, his pigs. That'll get the machetes flashing."

D.B. stressed the need to proceed cautiously with cultures we didn't understand, and Chang said, "Oh, enough of that travel guide suet. I was born here, for Christ's sake." There was a long silence—not counting the truck bottoming out several times in potholes—and I could almost hear the gears grinding in Chang's head. "Okay. It's Saturday. We'll swing by the bar, then hoof it over to the theater for *King Kong Meets Godzilla.*"

"Followed by Vivaldi's Opus No. 6 played on bamboo instruments, I suppose," D.B. said. Wabag didn't even have a store, so I was with D.B. in doubting this talk about its having a theater.

"I'm on the square here," Chang insisted. "It's been Kong and Godzilla every Saturday night for two years. But it's not the flick that's the draw, it's the Kanakas. Most of them think they're watching a documentary. I've seen them hike in all the way from the Gulf Province to see it."

We checked into the Wabag Lodge, an open-air dive with a running bath (the river), then headed for the bar. No Hard Rock Cafe, this was a cage of double chain link with the cashier and a stock of South Pacific Lager inside. We paid first, then the beers were slid through a little slot in the chain link. We hammered down a couple, then made for the theater, following a dark path to a small clearing in the otherwise impenetrable thicket.

The "theater" (the Wabag Ritz, as Chang called it) was a converted cement garage previously used to store Wabag's three old John Deere tractors. A noisy queue of Kanakas passed slowly through the tiny entrance. Dressed exclusively in ass-grass, they were obliged to check in their axes and machetes, receiving a numbered bottle cap to reclaim them. Several men, newcomers to the Ritz, were confused by this procedure, but were quickly pacified by an enormous native official at the door. He too wore the ass-grass, but also a creased khaki shirt and a red beret on his billowing bouffant. He flashed a wide smile when he saw Chang.

"Sainaman tru." This from the giant.

"Strongpela tru," Chang came back. The two exchanged a five-move handshake, then Chang turned toward D.B. and me. "Dispelas em i pren bilong me. Americans."

"Oh, how ya doing?" the giant said fluidly. "You blokes best grab a seat while you can."

We went in. One hundred and fifty natives were already pressed inside. Several benches were in place, but most Kanakas chose to squat in the oily dirt. The front wall was whitewashed. The ancient projector sat askew on a bamboo stand. The heat was withering, but the aroma could have turned the stomach of a granite statue. The natives' diet is almost exclusively forest tubers and shrubbery, and they continually pass a crippling wind, unabashed, and most sonorously. Blend that with knee-buckling body odor and the fetid stench of betel nut expectoration, then box it all in a ventless concrete sarcophagus and you have the Wabag Ritz.

"Swank joint, eh?" Chang chuckled.

"Probably no worse than the atmosphere on Mercury," I said. D.B. mentioned he was finding it just a little easier to breathe than when he had typhoid fever in Upper Volta.

"Pasim tok," the giant barked, and the crowd quieted. He flipped on the projector, which made a gnashing noise like someone feeding hubcaps into a wheat thresher. He compensated by turning the volume way up, which distorted the Japanese dialogue beyond anything human, but rendered King Kong that much more horrendous. As Kong stomped through Tokyo, swatting down skyscrapers and feasting on pedestrians, their legs flailing in his jagged teeth, dreadful shrieks issued from the mob, and many

Kanakas dove beneath the benches, cowering and trembling and babbling about the "bikpela monki, em i kaikai saipan man."

During the scene when Godzilla and Kong had it out, a fight erupted in the corner. Just as a free-for-all looked a certainty, a torpedo-busted mother of six squealing kids swung her bilum bag of spuds upside a Kanaka's head, and all eyes returned to the wall. Later, a courageous Kanaka stole up to the wall to "touch" Godzilla. He turned around, squinting into the light, and was instantly bombarded by sweet potatoes and betel nut husks. He screamed, the crowd howled, the giant barked, and the bushman bolted back to his bench.

The end credits rolled out and the wall went blank. A short silence was followed by shouts for more. The giant yelled, "No gat," but the mob didn't buy a word of it, so to avoid a sure riot, he simply rolled the film back in reverse. As King Kong backpedaled through Tokyo, withdrawing reconstituted pedestrians from his snapping jaws and placing them back onto the sidewalk, great cheers boomed from the crowd. More farting, more yelling, more spitting.

Over the next six days we met "Queen Gigi" of the Highlands, all two hundred kilos of her; were invited to dinner by the local police chief, and when we relished the tender meat, the chief told us we'd just dined on a stillborn boy and we believed him for two days. And at the party during the solar eclipse, D.B. drank so much raw cane liquor he passed out, and when I found him, a Kanaka was tattooing a cassowary bird on his back and had already tapped out the head—all but the beak. Then I got suckered into the Kanaka version of craps, involving thrown hornbill quills of different lengths. I'd won forty kina, but then kept losing and drinking and getting more pissed off and finally I lost it all, two months' wages to a toothless coffee farmer who kept his father's skull in a rusty powdered-milk tin.

But the queen and the chief's gag and even the tattoo all paled next to the feature presentation at the Wabag Ritz.

THE THREE WISHES

OR

THE MAN WHO LONGED TO SEE THE NIGHT OF POWER

from A Thousand Nights and A Night

A certain man had longed all his life to look upon the Night of Power, and one night it befell that he gazed at the sky and saw the angels, and Heaven's gates thrown open; and he beheld all things prostrating themselves before their Lord, each in its several stead. So he said to his wife, "Harkye, such an one, verily Allah hath shown me the Night of Power, and it hath been proclaimed to me, from the invisible world, that three prayers will be granted unto me; so I consult thee for counsel as to what shall I ask." Quoth she, "O man, the perfection of man and his delight is in his prickle; therefore do thou pray Allah to greaten thy yard and magnify it." So he lifted up his hands to heaven and said, "O Allah, greaten my yard and magnify it." Hardly had he spoken when his tool became as big as a column and he could neither sit nor stand nor move about nor even stir from his stead; and when he would have carnally known his wife, she fled before him from place to place. So he said to her, "O accursed woman, what is to be done? This is thy list, by reason of thy lust." She replied, "No, by Allah, I did not ask for this length and huge bulk, for which the gate of a street were too strait. Pray Heaven to make it less." So he raised his eyes to Heaven and said "O Allah, rid me of this thing and deliver me therefrom." And immediately his prickle disappeared altogether and he became clean smooth. When his wife saw this, she said, "I have no occasion for thee, now thou are become pegless as a eunuch, shaven and shorn;" and he answered her, saying, "All this comes of thine ill-omened counsel and thine imbecile judgment. I had three prayers accepted of Allah, wherewith I might have gotten me my good, both in this world and in the next, and now two wishes are gone in pure waste, by thy lewd will, and there remaineth but one." Quoth she, "Pray Allah the Most High to restore thee thy yard as it was." So he prayed to his Lord and his prickle was restored to its first estate. Thus the man lost his three wishes.

Excerpts From:
NO TIME FOR SERGEANTS
by Mac Hyman

(No Time for Sergeants *recounts the army adventures of Draftee Will Stockdale, of Georgia. Stockdale is willing, genial, incredibly strong—but not very bright, and unused to discipline of any kind. He is the nemesis of Sergeant King, whose effort to fob him off on permanent latrine duty culminates on the first episode reprinted here. The second episode takes place after Stockdale and his buddy, Ben, are assigned to practice missions, and involves a cast of characters equally engaging as King, but in different ways.* No Time for Sergeants *was published in October 1954*)

• • •

The next day for inspection I cleaned up everything real white, except the tops which warnt supposed to be white, and Sergeant King went pacing all around the place examining bunks and getting wrinkles out of them and things like that, and telling everybody how to act, and just what the officers would do and everything. He worried a good bit about inspection like that, and he explained it to everybody again, and it happened just like he said it would too. The door opened and some Lieutenants and the Captain and the Colonel come in, and Sergeant King called out "Attention!" and everybody stood real stiff like they warnt breathing, and the Lieutenants peeped and sniffed around here and there, and the Captain went around looking over the men in their fresh uniforms, but the Colonel, he didnt waste no time at all—he only glanced at things and headed right past, coming for the latrine where I was standing at attention by myself, just like Sergeant King said he would do.

And he really was the most interested in latrines of any man you ever seen in your life, He was a nice old fellow too, gray-headed with a little moustache and looked like an uncle of mine, but I knowed it warnt as my uncle hadnt been drafted that I had heered—anyhow, he headed right back for the latrine and went in and looked around, nodding his head and smiling, and seemed mighty pleased with it. And I was myself when I seen the look on his face and seen Sergeant King kind of cutting his eyes around at him. But I didnt want to take all the credit for myself, so when he come back by me on his way out, I said, "Colonel, I hope you like how we fixed up the latrine for you."

And when he turned to me and said, "What?" I said, "The reason it is so clean was mainly because of Sergeant King there. He's the one behind it all; I just done the cleaning. He said he had never seen a man in his life care more about latrines than you do, and that's the reason..."

"Attention!" the Captain yelled out. "You're at attention there!" and he come bounding over with his face all red like he was going to jump all over me.

But I didnt pay much attention to him because I warnt talking to him nohow, and besides the Colonel held up his hand at the Captain to shut him up, and then he looked at me for a while and asked me to go over what I had said again. So I did, and this time I really laid it on good too. I told him how Sergeant King had told me to clean it up so good because he had never seen a man in his life that would come back and stick his head right down in the bowls the way he done, and I think the Colonel kind of appreciated it too, because he looked around and said, "And which one is Sergeant King?"

So I pointed him out, though Sergeant King was right embarrassed and kind of white in the face, and the Colonel went over to speak with him for a minute. I couldnt make out what he said, though, because the Captain begun talking to me, and seemed like he had got kind of interested in the latrine himself. He asked me if I had been doing all the cleaning by myself, and I told him, "Yessir, I been cleaning it for about two weeks now. I'm the permanent latrine orderly."

"You mean you havent even started *classification* yet? You've been here two weeks and havent even *started* ... Oh Sergeant King, step over here a minute, will you, when the Colonel finished speaking with you."

So we all kind of gathered around, the Colonel and the Captain and the Lieutenants and Sergeant King and myself, and had a real nice chat about it. They wanted to know about what I had been doing and I told them about the latrine and how Sergeant King let me work there, and how at first I was on KP for a while, and how nice Sergeant King had been to me, not making me bother with classification but letting me help wash his car and all; and we kept talking about it, only Sergeant King didnt say much but kept his head ducked down and kept blushing and acting modest and everything—anyhow, we talked and talked—and finally they got ready to leave, and the Captain said, "King, you come over and wait in the office. I want to talk to you a little while," and Sergeant King come to attention and said, "Yessir," so it all seemed to come off all right. And they was about the nicest bunch of officers I had ever seen and must have knowed me from somewhere because just as they were leaving, the Captain looked at me and said, "You must be Stockdale."

And I said, "Yessir, that's right, but I dont recall meeting you . . ." but he didnt stay around no longer; he only turned to the Lieutenant and said, "That one's Stockdale," and the Lieutenant looked at me and said, "Oh, yeah," and I said, "Yessir, that's right, but I dont recall meeting . . ." but they were already headed out about that time.

Anyhow, you could never tell how Sergeant King would feel about things, as changeable as he was, and when he come back from talking with the Captain, he was most *wild-looking* in a way. He stood in his room and kept blinking his eyes and shaking his head like he didnt even know I was there. "You didnt have to do it," he finally said. "You really didnt have to do that."

"I know it," I said. "But I didnt see no sense in me taking all the credit when it was your idea and all. You done a lot for me and I though I could help out some and . . ."

But he kept shaking his head, and said, "Yes, but did you think that would be helping . . ." and then he stopped and rubbed his hands over his face and said, "Yes, I guess you would. I'm not surprised at all. But look here now, you dont have to help me out no more, see? I get along all right here. I got three stripes and my own barracks and I dont really need no help. You've done enough for me already. Look, you help somebody else out for a while. Look, I know a loud-mouthed, low-down, four-striper over in the orderly room, why dont you help *him* out a little bit? Why . . . ?" But then he waved his hand like he didnt want to talk about it no more, and I said I would if I got the chance, but he waved his hand again and turned back around and said, "Look, Will, just forget everything else now. The main thing now is to get you *classified*. That's something we've *got* to do."

And then he seemed to get all upset about that too. He got to pacing up and down talking about it, seeming right anxious about it, and looking all worried again. So I tried to calm him down a bit; I said it probably didnt amount to much and that there really warnt that much to worry about because I liked the latrine fine and had just as soon stay right there as long as I was on the field.

But that seemed to upset him too. He said, "No Will, no! You wouldnt want to spend the rest of your hitch here, would you? You want to get out and do something. Nosir, what we want to do is get you classified and shipped out of here, because the Captain said that if you didnt, you would stay right here and . . . Look, Will, if it's the last thing we ever do, I think we ought to get you classified. It's the *only* thing."

"Well, I was only thinking about the latrine and helping you out and . . ."

But he was the most upset I ever seen him. He said, "Nosir! Nosir! Absolutely not! The Captain said . . ." and then he got all jumbled up with it all. He shouted "Nosir!" a few more times, and then, "They'll ship you a thousand miles away from here!" and a lot of other stuff like that, getting more and more upset. And finally he wore himself out and just laid down on the bunk and covered up his face with his arms, upset the way he was. So just as I was leaving, I said, "Well, if they do ship me a thousand miles away from here, I might manage to hitch a ride back every once in a while," but it didnt do no good. He only moaned, his face still covered up and didnt answer me at all.

• • •

After we got assigned to gunnery, me and Ben both got to be airmans-third-class, which means you wear a stripe on your arm, only we didnt get to wear it long because of this Captain that was in charge of our crew in transition. He was pilot of the plane and was always real particular, wanting you to wear neckties and such most of the time, which I didnt care nothing about. Anyhow, he stopped me and Ben up town one day and I didnt have my tie on, and we had a few words about that when I tried to explain to him how it was, which I found out later I warnt supposed to do—Ben said all I was supposed to do was stand there and say, "No excuse, sir," which sounded like a kind of foolish way to talk to a man—so one thing led to another and we was recruits again; and besides that he changed us off his crew and put us in another crew. And Ben didnt like that too much because he said we was now on the sorriest crew on the base. He said everybody knowed it was the worst crew there, but I didnt much think so myself because I got along with them pretty good. They was real easygoing compared to the other one; it didnt make much difference with them whether you showed up for a mission or not. Lieutenant Bridges was the pilot and he was a Reserve and was the only one of the officers I knowed much at first because the planes was so monstrously big and because we flew in the back and they flew in the front so that we didnt see much of the others, and didnt know them usually when we did. But Lieutenant Bridges was a mighty easygoing fellow and didnt care much what you done; he went around most of the time with his eyes about half-opened and half-closed, just kind of dragging himself around like he was walking in his sleep, only he just seemed that way, I think; he warnt really asleep but probably only half drunk, even though it was kind of hard to tell the difference most of the time. And as far as I was concerned, I had ruther been on his crew than the first one because he was so easy to work for. If you took it in your head you didnt want to go on a mission, he never would notice you warnt there nohow. I mean like this one fellow we had; he didnt fly hardly any and one day when he come out to the plane, Lieutenant Bridges didnt remember him and wouldnt let him fly with us until he went back to Operations and got a card showing he was supposed to be on our crew.

Anyhow, Sergeant King had got back to being a sergeant again by that time and had got himself a job in the Orderly Room, and me and Ben hung around a good bit, not doing much but going on practice missions, and Ben finally quit worrying about losing his stripe, and we had a right nice time. Ben still didnt like the crew much—he was mighty disappointed in them most of the time and said it was a good thing most of the officers warnt like them and all like that, but he liked flying a lot, so we went on most of the missions, not skipping them the way about half the crew did. And I didnt mind it much myself—it warnt much trouble because there warnt nothing to do in the back of the plane but sleep or play cards or set there and watch the country go under you. Finally I got a checkerboard and took that along, and me and Ben and this other fellow took turns playing each other, only the other fellow didnt play much because he was working on a model airplane that he took along with him. We never did get to know him too good, though, because he finally just quit coming altogether, and I guess he must have dropped off the crew because we didnt see him around nowhere for a long time.

Anyhow, there warnt much to it; when we was scheduled for a mission, me and Ben went and crawled in the back of the plane, and when it landed, we crawled back out, and never had anything to say to anybody except sometimes when Lieutenant Bridges would call back to see if anybody else was around, and I was kind of enjoying it. And then one day I happened to meet the co-pilot up in Operations, which was a right peculiar thing because we was just standing there talking together and his voice sounded familiar and he said mine did too, and finally we found out we was on the same crew together. His name was Lieutenant Gardella and he seemed like a real nice fellow, and when I asked him what they done up in the front of the plane, he said, "Nothing much. What do y'all do in the back?"

So I told him about the checkers and the cards that we played sometimes and he said that sounded mighty good to him and that he would come back and play with us sometimes, and I told him I would like to have him and that I wanted him to meet Ben besides. I asked him what his job was and he said, "Oh, I do different things. Mainly, I just let the wheels up and down and I stick to that pretty much as I dont care to take on anything more right now."

"How long you been letting them up and down?"

"A pretty good while," he said. "About six weeks now, ever since I got out of cadets. Next time we fly I'm going to let the flaps up and down too. Say, why dont you come up front and fly with us next time? Why dont you ask Bridges about it?"

"Well, that's mighty nice of you. I'd sho' like to see you let them wheels up and down."

"Sure," he said. "I'll show you all about it."

He was a real obliging kind of fellow that way and you wouldnt think he was an officer at all just to look at him—he looked like he was only about thirteen years old and you would probably think he was a Boy Scout instead of an officer if you seen him, only he always had this big cigar in his mouth and usually didnt seem real sober neither, which of course aint like most Boy Scouts as they usually seem right sober most of the time.

So I went out and finally found Lieutenant Bridges in the BOQ and he was laying down on his bunk and I had to stand around a while before I could tell whether he was asleep or awake with his eyes half open the way they always was, but finally he set up and looked at me, and I told him what I wanted. And he said, "Look here, you cant just go around flying here and there. Why dont you ask your own pilot?"

And I told him he was my pilot, and so he looked at me for a while and finally said, "Oh, yeah, I thought I had seen you around somewhere before. What did you say your name was now?"

So we talked for a while and he said I could ride up front with them on the next trip, and then I asked about Ben, and he said, "Ben who?" and I explained to him that Ben was another one of his gunners, and he said it was all right by him, that it didnt make no difference to him one way or the other.

But when I went back and told Ben about it, Ben said, "No, I'll stay in the back where I'm supposed to stay. I never seen officers care as little about things as this bunch does. I wish we had never got off the other crew myself."

So I told him I would ride in the back too, but he said, "No, there aint any use in that. After all, the pilot is in charge of the plane and what he says goes, I guess, even if he dont seem to know what he is talking about half the time."

But they warnt all that bad, I didnt think, and I really enjoyed watching them work when I flew up front. We took off that day about dark and Lieutenant Bridges got the plane off the ground real good and Lieutenant Gardella let the wheels up and done a right good job of it too, right smack up in the sides like he had been borned doing it; we went skimming out over the end of the runway and then Lieutenant Gardella got out a cigar and stuck it in his mouth and rared back and begun reading a magazine, while Lieutenant Bridges flew back over the field and then set it on the automatic, and then propped his feet up and leaned his seat back to go to sleep. I watched it all and it seemed like they done right good, and then I went back to talk with Lieutenant Kendall, the engineer, only he said he was sleepy and was getting his parachute under his head and sticking his feet out in the aisle trying to get comfortable. So I finally went back and set in the radio operator's seat, because he hadnt showed up, and watched Lieutenant Cover while he navigated; and he was the one I wished Ben could have seen because he was probably the hardest-working man I ever seen in my life. He was bounding all over the back of the plane navigating even before it was over the end of the runway, peeping down tubes and looking out the window and writing things down on maps that he had scattered all over the desk, then grabbing up one of them three watches that he had scattered around and checking the time, and writing that down, and then taking this camera-looking thing he had, and running back to the dome and pointing it out at the stars that was just coming out, and then running back to write that down too. He wrote so fast and so hard that twice the lead flew off the pencil and flipped across the plane and nearly hit me in the eye; and another time he snatched up a map that had this weight on it that sailed across the desk and caught me right beside the head; so I got up and moved down a ways after that, as it did seem right dangerous being close to him working that hard, but I still watched him a good while and got a kick out of it.

Anyhow, I wished Ben could have seen it the way he went at things; he was so busy most of the time he wouldnt even talk to me. Most people that work hard usually like to talk about it a good bit, but when I asked him where he was navigating to, he snapped real quick, "Biloxi, Mississippi. Dont bother me, I'm busy," and wouldnt even look at me. After a little bit, we was well on the way and it was dark and the plane was quiet the way it gets at night, with only the sounds of the engines and no lights to speak of except little blue dials and the lamp that come down over Lieutenant Cover's head; but watching him work was enough to wear you out, so I got a little bit sleepy, and must have dozed off for a good while because when I woke up there was a big disturbance going on with people walking around and talking, and I didnt know what was going on.

Anyhow, I woke up and felt the plane going in these big circles, and then I looked over to the desk and there was Lieutenant Bridges standing holding one of the maps in his hand and looking at it, and Lieutenant Cover arguing with him, rattling papers around trying to show him how he had figured this and that. Lieutenant Kendall was setting over there watching them with his chin propped up on his hands, and Lieutenant Gardella was up front flying the plane in these big circles, looking around every once in a while to see what was going on with the big cigar stuck out of his mouth; they was talking loud and everybody seemed real interested in it, and it seemed like Lieutenant Bridges knowed a lot about navigation himself even though he was the pilot. He was waving the map around saying, "I dont care what your figures show. I guess I can look out the window and see, cant I?"

"Well, you just check the figures for yourself," Lieutenant Cover said. "I got a fix about thirty minutes ago and that showed us right here, and thirty minutes later, we're supposed to be right here. You can check every figure down there. I figured that position by Dead Reckoning and I figured it thirty minutes from that fix, and I know it's right!"

But Lieutenant Bridges kept on shaking his head and saying, "Well, by God, I can see, cant I? I can look right out the window and see, cant I?"

So they talked a good bit about navigation that way and both took a lot of interest in it, it seemed like. Lieutenant Kendall was setting back there listening to the whole thing and he was right interested too, even though he was the engineer, and so I stepped back there and asked him what the discussion was all about. And he said, "What do you think it's about? They're lost again naturally. I been in this plane seven times and five of them we been lost. All I know is how much gas we got and if they want to know that, I'll be glad to tell them, but I aint going to worry about it anymore. They can ditch the plane or jump out for all I care; the only thing I know is about how much gas we got."

Then Lieutenant Gardella called back and asked how much gas did we have, and Lieutenant Kendall said, "Tell him we can fly another forty minutes. I dont want to talk with him because every time we do, we get in an argument over where we are, and I'm tired of talking about it."

"I know what you mean," I said. "I dont like to argue about things neither, but it is good to see everybody taking such an interest in things; old Ben would be surprised to see it."

"Who is Ben?"

"He's one of the gunners," I said. "He rides in the back of the plane."

"Well," Lieutenant Kendall said. "I hope he knows how to use a parachute."

"Sho'," I said. "I bet Ben knows about as much about parachutes as anybody you ever seen."

Anyhow we chatted a while and then I went back and listened to Lieutenant Bridges and Lieutenant Cover some more. Lieutenant Cover was still talking about his DR position where he said we ought to be; he turned to Lieutenant Bridges and said, "Well, who's been navigating, you or me? I got a fix no more'n thirty minutes ago and that means our DR position is right here, about a hundred miles out over the Gulf of Mexico..."

And then Lieutenant Bridges come in with his side of the argument, saying, "Well, I might not have been navigating but I got eyes in my head, and I guess I can look out the window right now and see we're circling over a town half the size of New York; and according to this map or none I ever saw in my life, there aint a town at all in the middle of the Gulf of Mexico, much less one half the size of New York and..."

"Well, just look then," Lieutenant Cover said. "Dont argue with me, just look. You can check every figure I got here. My DR position puts..."

"Well, I dont care anything about that," Lieutenant Bridges said. "All I want to know is what town we're circling over, and if you can tell me that, we can land this thing because we cant fly here all night long while you try to tell me there is a town of that size in the middle of the Gulf of Mexico!"

So they took on that way for a while, and then Lieutenant Gardella and Lieutenant Kendall had a pretty good argument about one of the engines going out; so they discussed that a good while too until Lieutenant Kendall said, "Well, there's not any sense in arguing about it; I'm going to feather the thing." And after a little bit, they changed positions, and Lieutenant Bridges came up front and looked out and seen that one of the engines warnt working, and went back to see Lieutenant Kendall and they had a long talk over the engine being feathered too. Lieutenant Bridges said, "You are not supposed to go around feathering engines like that. I'm the one that's supposed to feather the engine. I'm the pilot, aint I?"

"Yeah, but you was too busy trying to navigate the plane when you're supposed to be up there flying it and..."

"All right," Lieutenant Bridges said, "But at least you could have told me we had lost an engine. I am the pilot, aint I?"

So they talked about that a good while too, and I set back and watched and listened, only I must have dozed off again because when I woke up, we was coming in for a landing. We hit and bounced once pretty hard so that I got throwed halfway across the plane, and then bounced again so that it throwed me back where I started from, but then I grabbed on and didnt get throwed no more on the rest of the bounces. We taxied up the runway with the wheels squeaking and finally stopped and started getting out, but nobody was talking much by then except Lieutenant Gardella—he kept telling Lieutenant Bridges that he thought the third bounce was the smoothest of all, but Lieutenant Bridges didnt seem to care about talking about it none, and I noticed in a minute that none of the others did either.

Anyhow, we got out and they had this truck waiting for us and we got on that, and nobody was discussing nothing by this time, and I was right sorry for that because I wanted Ben to hear them because they was right interesting to listen to. But everybody just set there and then Lieutenant Cover come out with all his maps and everything folded up, and he got in and didnt say a word to nobody either. The truck finally started up and we headed across the ramp with everybody real quiet until finally Lieutenant Bridges leaned over and tapped Lieutenant Cover on the shoulder and said, "Look, Cover, I dont mean to run this thing into the ground, but I would appreciate it if you would try to find out where this place is. I mean if it is in the middle of the Gulf of Mexico, we've damn well discovered something."

And then Lieutenant Cover said, "Well, the way you fly, it's a wonder we didnt end up there anyhow."

So we drove up and got off and everybody stood around for a while hemming and hawing, and Lieutenant Bridges went over and asked Lieutenant Cover again if he had figured out where we was, and Lieutenant Cover said, "I thought you was the one who knew so much about it. If you want to find out, why dont you ask the driver?"

But then Lieutenant Bridges said, "Ask the driver? You expect me to land a plane and then go over and ask a truck driver where I landed it?" and got right stubborn about it. But then he turned to me and said, "Hey, what was your name now?"

"Stockdale," I said.

"Look, Stockdale," he said. "How about scouting around here somewhere and see if you cant find out what place this is, will you? Be kind of casual about it, you know."

So I went down the way and asked a fellow and he told me Houston, Texas, and I come back and told Lieutenant Bridges and he seemed to feel much better about things then. "Well, Houston aint such a bad town after all," he said. "By gosh, Cover, you're getting better every day. You didn't miss the field but by about four-hundred and fifty miles this time."

Then Lieutenant Cover said, "Well, what I figgered was that you would bounce the rest of the way—it looked like it from the way we landed . . ."

And then Lieutenant Bridges had something to say to that, and after a while they begun squabbling a little bit, which I didnt like to hear. Me and Ben stood around waiting while they went at it and Ben said to me, "I never heered a bunch of officers argue so much in my life!"

"Yeah, Ben, they do now, but you ought to have been in the front of that plane and seen the way they worked. That was something else. If you could have seen that, you would have thought a lot more of them. Why, I'll bet they are about as good a crew as you can find, when they're sober like that."

"Which aint often," Ben said.

Anyhow, I hated for Ben to hear the squabbling and kept on talking to him until they had finished up with it because he got so disgusted about things like that. But they was finally finished; all of them heading across the ramp except Lieutenant Cover who had lost the argument because they had all jumped on him together before it was over—he was getting all his charts and stuff up and mumbling to himself. And I felt right sorry for him the way he had lost out on the argument and everything; I went over to him and said, "Well, I wouldnt worry about it none. I dont see how it amounts to too much. I had just as soon land at this field as any other one, and we aint going to be here but one day nohow . . ."

But he was right down on things and turned around and looked at me like he was almost mad with me, and said, "Look, do you want to check my figures? Do you want to check them and see for yourself? I got them all right here!"

"Well, I dont know nothing about it," I said. "If you say they're right, I guess they is."

"I can show you my DR position," he said. "It shows us right out in the Gulf."

"Well, I wouldnt know about that," I said. "If you say your DR position is out in the Gulf, I reckon that's where it is all right. How long do you expect it to be out there?"

But he was pretty much down on things; he turned away and stomped off without even answering me—nothing you could say would make him feel any better.

From:
A Double Barrelled Detective Story
by Mark Twain

Just after the turn of the century, a steady flow of Sherlock Holmes stories swept across the Atlantic to captivate the American audience. Perhaps bristling at a foreigner horning onto his claim, Mark Twain parodied the famous sleuth from Baker Street in A Double Barrelled Detective Story. *But it wasn't the story so much as a single word in the first paragraph of Part IV that caused a ruckus. The paragraph runs:*

It was a crisp and spicy morning in early October. The lilacs and laburnums, lit with the glory-fires of autumn, hung burning and flashing in the upper air, a fairy bridge provided by kind Nature for the wingless wild things that have their homes in the tree-tops and would visit together; the larch and the pomegranate flung their purple and yellow flames in brilliant broad splashes along the slanting sweep of the woodland; the sensuous fragrance of innumerable deciduous flowers rose upon the swooning atmosphere; far in the empty sky a solitary esophagus slept upon motionless wing; everywhere brooded stillness, serenity, and the peace of God.

Shortly after the publication of A Double Barrelled Detective Story, *the following letter appeared in the April 12, 1903 edition of the Springfield* Republican:

To the Editor of the *Republican*:

One of your citizens has asked me a question about the "esophagus," and I wish to answer him through you. This is in the hope that the answer will get around, and save me some penmanship, for I have already replied to the same question more than several times, and am not getting as much holiday as I ought to have.

I published a short story lately, and it was in that I put the esophagus. I will say privately that I expected it to bother some people—in fact, that was the intention—but the harvest has been larger than I was calculating upon. The esophagus has gathered in the guilty and the innocent alike, whereas I was only fishing for the innocent—the innocent and confiding. I knew a few of these would write and ask me; that would give me bit little trouble; but I was not expecting that the wise and learned would call upon me for succor. However, that has happened, and it is time for me to speak up and stop the inquiries if I can, for letter-writing is not restful to me, and I am not having so much fun out of this thing as I counted on. That you may understand the situation I will insert a couple of sample inquiries. The first is from a public instructor in the Philippines:

> Santa Cruz, *Ilocos, Sur, P.I.*
> February 13, 1902
> My Dear Sir, I have just been reading the first part of your latest story, entitled *A Double Barreled Detective Story*, and am very much delighted with it. In Part IV, page 264, *Harper's Magazine* for January, occurs this passage: "Far in the empty sky a solitary 'esophagus' slept upon motionless wing; everywhere brooded stillness, serenity, and the peace of God." Now there is one word I do not understand, namely, "esophagus." My only work of reference is the *Standard Dictionary*, but that fails to explain the meaning. If you can spare the time, I would be glad to have the meaning cleared up, as I consider the passage a very touching and beautiful one. It may seem foolish to you, but consider my lack of means away out in the northern part of Luzon.
> Yours very truly . . .

Do you notice? Nothing in the paragraph disturbed him but that one word. It shows that paragraph was most ably constructed for the deception it was intended to put upon the reader. It was my intention that it should read plausibly, and it is now plain that it does; it was my intention that it should be emotional and touching, and you see, yourself, that it fetched this public instructor. Alas, if I had but left that one treacherous word out, I should have scored! scored everywhere; and the paragraph would have slidden through every reader's sensibilities like oil, and left not a suspicion behind.

The other sample inquiry is from a professor in a New England university. It contains one naughty word (which I cannot bear to suppress), but he is not in the theological department, so it is no harm:

> Dear Mr. Clemens: "Far in the empty sky a solitary esophagus slept upon motionless wing."

It is not often I get a chance to read much periodical literature, but I have just gone through at this belated period, with much gratification and edification, your *Double Barreled Detective Story*.

But what in hell is an esophagus? I keep one myself, but it never sleeps in the air or anywhere else. My profession is to deal with words, and esophagus interested me the moment I lighted upon it. But as a companion of my youth used to say, "I'll be eternally, co-eternally cussed" if I can make it out. It is a joke, or I an ignoramus?

Between you and me, I was almost ashamed of having fooled that man, but for pride's sake I was not going to say so. I wrote and told him it was a joke—and that is what I am now saying to my Springfield inquirer.

I have confessed. I am sorry—partially. I will not do so any more-for the present. Don't ask me any more question; let the esophagus have a rest—on his same old motionless wing.

—Mark Twain

The First Piano in a Mining Camp
by Sam Davis

Mr. Samuel Davis was formerly a reporter for the San Francisco Argonaut, *and later the editor of the Carson* Appeal.

In 1858—it might have been five years earlier or later; this is not history for the public school—there was a little camp about ten miles from Pioche, occupied by upwards of three hundred miners, every one of whom might have packed his prospecting implements and left for more inviting fields any time before sunset. When the day was over, these men did not rest from their labors, like the honest New England agriculturist, but sang, danced, gambled, and shot each other, as the mood seized them.

One evening the report spread along the main street (which was the only street) that three men had been killed at Silver Reef, and that the bodies were coming in. Presently a lumbering old conveyance labored up the hill, drawn by a couple of horses, well worn out with their pull. The cart contained a good-sized box, and no sooner did its outlines become visible, through the glimmer of a stray light here and there, than it began to affect the idlers. Death always enforces respect, and even though no one had caught sight of the remains, the crowd gradually became subdued, and when the horses came to a standstill, the cart was immediately surrounded. The driver, however, was not in the least impressed with the solemnity of his commission.

"All there?" asked one.

"Haven't examined. Guess so."

The driver filled his pipe, and lit it as he continued:

"Wish the bones and load had gone over the grade!"

A man who had been looking on stepped up to the man at once.

"I don't know who you have in that box, but if they happen to be any friends of mine, I'll lay you alongside."

"We can mighty soon see," said the teamster, coolly. "Just burst the lid off, and if they happen to be the men you want, I'm here."

The two looked at each other for a moment, and then the crowd gathered a little closer, anticipating trouble.

"I believe that dead men are entitled to good treatment, and when you talk about hoping to see corpses go over a bank, all I have to say is, that it will be better for you if the late lamented ain't my friends."

"We'll open the box. I don't take back what I've said, and if my language don't suit your ways of thinking, I guess I can stand it."

With these words the teamster began to pry up the lid. He got a board off, and then pulled out some old rags. A strip of something dark, like rosewood, presented itself.

"Eastern coffins, by thunder!" said several, and the crowd looked quite astonished.

Some more boards flew up, and the man who was ready to defend his friend's memory shifted his weapon a little. The cool manner of the teamster had so irritated him that he had made up his mind to pull his weapon at the first sight of the dead, even if the deceased was his worst and oldest enemy. Presently the whole of the box cover was off, and the teamster, clearing away the packing revealed to the astonished group the top of something which puzzled all alike.

"Boys," said he, "this is a pianner."

A general shout of laughter went up, and the man who had been so anxious to enforce respect for the dead muttered something about feeling dry, and the keeper of the nearest bar was several ounces better off by the time the boys had given the joke all the attention it called for.

Had a dozen dead men been in the box, their presence in the camp could not have occasioned half the excitement that the arrival of that lonely piano caused. By the next morning it was known that the instrument was to grace a hurdy-gurdy saloon, owned by Tom Goskin, the leading gambler in the place. It took nearly a week to get this wonder on its legs, and the owner was the proudest individual in the State. It rose gradually from a recumbent to an upright position amid a confusion of tongues, after the manner of the Tower of Babel.

Of course everybody knew just how such an instrument should be put up. One knew where the "off hind leg" should go, and another was posted on the "front piece."

Scores of men came to the place every day to assist.

"I'll put the bones in good order."

"If you want the wires tuned up, I'm the boy."

"I've got music to feed it for a month."

Another brought a pair of blankets for a cover, and all took the liveliest interest in it. It was at last in a condition for business.

"It's been showin' its teeth all the week. We'd like to have it spin out something."

Alas! there wasn't a man to be found who could play upon the instrument. Goskin began to realize that he had a losing speculation on his hands. He had a fiddler, and a Mexican who thrummed a guitar. A pianist would have made his orchestra complete. One day a three-card monte player told a friend confidentially that he could "knock any amount of music out of the piano, if he only had it alone a few hours, to get his hand in." This report spread about the camp, but on being questioned he vowed that he didn't know a note of music. It was noted, however, as a suspicious circumstance, that he often hung about the instrument, and looked upon it longingly, like a hungry man gloating over a beefsteak in a restaurant window. There was no doubt but that this man had music in his soul, perhaps in his fingers' ends, but did not dare to make trial of his strength after the rules of harmony had suffered so many years of neglect. So the fiddler kept on with his jigs, and the greasy Mexican pawed his discordant guitar, but no man had the nerve to touch the piano. There were, doubtless, scores of men in the camp who would have given ten ounces of gold dust to have half an hour alone with it, but every man's nerve shrank from the jeers which the crowd would shower upon him should his first attempt prove a failure. It got to be generally understood that the hand which first essayed to draw music from the keys must not slouch its work.

• • •

It was Christmas Eve, and Goskin, according to his custom, had decorated his gambling hell with sprigs of mountain cedar, and a shrub whose crimson berries did not seem a bad imitation of English holly. The piano was covered with evergreens, and all that was wanting to completely fill the cup of Goskin's contentment was a man to play the instrument.

"Christmas night, and no piano-pounder," he said. "This is a nice country for a Christian to live in."

Getting a piece of paper, he scrawled the words:

$20 Reward
To a compitant Pianer Player.

This he stuck up on the music-rack, and, though the inscription glared at the frequenters of the room until midnight, it failed to draw any musician from his shell.

So the merry-making went on; the hilarity grew apace. Men danced and sang to the music of the squeaky fiddle and worn-out guitar, as the jolly crowd within tried to drown the howling of the storm without. Suddenly they became aware of the presence of a white-haired man, crouching near the fire-place. His garments—such as were left—were wet with melting snow, and he had a half-starved, half-crazed expression. He held his thin, trembling hands toward the fire, and the light of the blazing wood made them almost transparent. He looked about him once in a while, as if in search of something, and his presence cast such a chill over the place that gradually the sound of the revelry was hushed, and it seemed that this waif of the storm had brought in with it all of the gloom and coldness of the warring elements. Goskin, mixing up a cup of hot egg-nog, advanced and remarked cheerily:

"Here, stranger, brace up! This is the real stuff."

The man drained the cup, smacked his lips, and seemed more at home.

"Been prospecting, eh? Out in the mountains—caught in the storm! Lively night, this!"

"Pretty bad," said the man.

"Must feel pretty dry?"

The man looked at his streaming clothes and laughed, as if Goskin's remark was a sarcasm.

"How long out?"

"Four days."

"Hungry?"

The man rose up, and walking over to the lunch counter, fell to work upon some roast bear, devouring it like an wild animal would have done. As meat and drink and warmth began to permeate the stranger, he seemed to expand and lighten up. His features lost their pallor, and he grew more and more content with the idea that he was not in the grave. As he underwent these changes, the people about him got merrier and happier, and threw off the temporary feeling of depression which he had laid upon them.

"Do you always have your place decorated like this?" he finally asked of Goskin.

"This is Christmas Eve," was the reply.

The stranger was startled.

"December twenty-fourth, sure enough."

"That's the way I put it up, pard."

"When I was in England I always kept Christmas. But I had forgotten that this was the night. I've been wandering about in the mountains until I've lost track of the feasts of the church."

Presently his eye fell upon the piano.

"Where's the player?" he asked.

"Never had any," said Goskin, blushing at the expression.

"I used to play when I was young."

Goskin almost fainted at the admission.

"Stranger, do tackle it, and give us a tune! Nary man in this camp ever had the nerve to wrestle with that music box." His pulse beat faster, for he feared that the man would refuse.

"I'll do the best I can," he said.

There was no stool, but seizing a candle-box, he drew it up and seated himself before the instrument. It only required a few seconds for a hush to come over the room.

"That old coon is going to give the thing a rattle."

The sight of a man at the piano was something so unusual that even the faro-dealer, who was about to take in a fifty-dollar bet on the tray, paused and did not reach for the money. Men stopped drinking, with the glasses at their lips. Conversation appeared to have been struck with a sort of paralysis, and cards were no longer shuffled.

The old man brushed back his long white locks, looked up to the ceiling, half closed his eyes, and in a mystic sort of reverie passed his fingers over the keys. He touched but a single note, yet the sound thrilled the room. It was the key to his improvisation, and as he wove his chords together the music laid its spell upon every ear and heart. He felt his way along the keys, like a man treading uncertain paths; but he gained confidence as he progressed, and presently bent to his work like a master. The instrument was not in exact tune, but the ears of his audience, through long disuse, did not detect anything radically wrong. They heard a succession of grand chords, a suggestion of paradise, melodies here and there, and it was enough.

"See him counter with his left!" said an old rough, enraptured.

"He calls the tune every time on the upper end of the board," responded a man with a stack of chips in his hand.

The player wandered off into the old ballads they had heard at home. All the sad and melancholy and touching songs that came up like dreams of childhood, this unknown player drew from the keys. His hands kneaded their hearts like dough, and squeezed out tears as from a wet sponge. As the strains flowed one upon the other, they saw their homes of the long ago reared again; they were playing once more where the apple blossoms sank through the soft air to join the violets on the green turf of the old New England states; they saw the glories of the Wisconsin maples and the haze of the Indian summer blending their hues together; they recalled the heather of Scottish hills, the white cliffs of Britain, and heard the sullen roar of the sea, as it beat upon their memories, vaguely. Then came all the old Christmas carols, such as they had sung in church thirty years before; the subtle music that brings up the glimmer of wax tapers, the solemn shrines, the evergreen, holly, mistletoe, and surpliced choirs. Then the remorseless performer planted his final stab in every heart with *Home, Sweet Home*.

When the player ceased, the crowd slunk away from him. There was no more revelry and devilment left in his audience. Each man wanted to sneak off to his cabin and write the old folks a letter. The day was breaking as the last man left the place, and the player, laying his head down on the piano, fell asleep.

"I say, pard," said Goskin, "Don't you want a little rest?"

"I feel tired," the old man said. "Perhaps you'll let me rest here for the matter of a day or so."

He walked behind the bar, where some old blankets were lying, and stretched himself upon them.

"I feel pretty sick. I guess I won't last long. I've got a brother down in the ravine—his name's Driscoll. He don't know I'm here. Can you get him before morning. I'd like to see his face once before I die."

Goskin started at the mention of the name. He knew Driscoll well.

"He your brother? I'll have him here in half an hour."

As he dashed out into the storm the musician pressed his hand to his side and groaned. Goskin heard the word "Hurry!" and sped down the ravine to Driscoll's cabin. It was quite light in the room when the two men returned. Driscoll was pale as death.

"My God! I hope he's alive! I wronged him when we lived in England, twenty years ago."

They saw the old man had drawn the blankets over his face. The two stood a moment, awed by the thought that he might be dead. Goskin lifted the blanket, and pulled it down astonished. There was no one there!

"Gone!" cried Driscoll wildly.

"Gone!" echoed Goskin, pulling out his cash-drawer. "Ten thousand dollars in the sack, and the Lord knows how much loose change in the drawer!"

The next day the boys got out, followed a horse's tracks through the snow, and lost them in the trail leading towards Pioche.

There was a man missing from the camp. It was the three-card monte man, who used to deny point-blank that he could play the scale. One day they found a wig of white hair, and called to mind when the "stranger" had pushed those locks back when he looked toward the ceiling for inspiration, on the night of December 24, 1858.

You Drive, Dear
by Fred S. Tobey

When Charity Tisdale told her husband she wanted to learn to drive an automobile, she knew he would insist on teaching her himself, not because of any solicitude as to the quality of the instruction but to save money. George Tisdale was a miser, a skinflint, a thoroughgoing penny-pincher. At least that is what Charity would have said had you asked her.

And he did teach her himself, or at least he tried. It was not easy, for Charity was careless, witless and empty-headed. At least, that is what George would have told you had you asked him. He often told Charity without being asked.

From this you will gather that the first bloom of love and affection had departed from the Tisdale marriage, and something resembling antipathy had taken its place. However, though each was often heard to say, in response to some word or action, "I could kill you for that," it is not likely that either had any conscious intention of doing away with the other.

But one night opportunity flaunted itself so brazenly before Charity that she could not overlook it. They had been to a party in a neighboring town, and George had drunk more than he could conveniently hold. In the old days, knowing he would have to drive home, George would have been more cautious; but lately he had fallen into the habit of letting down the bars of restraint, knowing that Charity, now at long last a licensed driver, would take the wheel if necessary. When they left their friends' house, George could barely walk, let alone drive.

On the winding road through the South Hills, George was dismayed suddenly to find that he was going to be sick. He demanded of his wife that she pull over to the side of the road immediately.

The area was undergoing scenic improvements, and the usual wooden barrier at the far side of a small field where the terrain dropped away to the valley below had been replaced temporarily by sawhorses with flashing lights. However, there was plenty of space and George's urgency seemed to be great, so Charity quickly pulled the car off the road and brought the sedan to a stop.

Bright moonlight illuminated the valley with a lovely radiance that was completely lost on George as he steadied himself with one hand on a sawhorse. Nature's beauties were lost, too, upon his wife, for as she watched George with distaste it occurred to her quite suddenly that only a little push would be needed to send him careening into the void. Quite on impulse she left the car and administered the push, making it an extra good one just in case. With an exclamation of astonishment, George went over the edge and disappeared.

Not a headlight was to be seen in either direction, so, since there seemed to be no reason to hurry, Charity thought she might as well see just what had become of George. Cautiously, because of her fear of high places, she went to the edge and peered over. Yes, there he was, and his position on the moonlit rocks far below left no doubt of the success of her act. There had not been a tuft or a twig to show his tumbling descent through two hundred feet of clear mountain air. Since death must have been instantaneous, Charity did not even feel squeamish about letting her eyes rest on the distant body while she recalled, for a long, long moment, just a few of the innumerable reasons why her husband had so richly deserved his fate.

• • •

Charity's sister Sarah poured a little more tea for Detective-Sergeant Rourke. She had been having her tea when he arrived.

"Well," she said, "You can keep on asking questions as long as you like and I'll do the best I can to answer them, because you're a police officer, but I just don't see what earthly help you're going to get from anything I can tell you."

"There's the matter of trying to get at a motive somehow," said the sergeant patiently. "Find a motive and you've solved the case, more often than not. We're still not satisfied on the motive and we've been hoping something you would tell us might help."

"They were fighting all the time. I told you that."

"Yes. True enough. But that doesn't quite seem to explain everything, as I think you can see. What did they usually quarrel about?"

"Oh, it didn't make any difference to them; they could fight about one thing just as easy as another. It was something different every day and twice on Sundays. If she said it was going to rain, he'd say it was going to be fine, and off they'd go again, hammer and tongs."

"It's a puzzling case," said Sergeant Rourke. "I'd be glad enough to call it a traffic accident or a double suicide and consider it closed, if I could just figure how the pair of them could have got out of the car while it was falling through the air. It hit the rocks farther down than they did, there's no doubt about that."

The sergeant rose and picked up his hat.

"Well, I'll be running along now," said he, "but I may be back again, so if you think of anything, keep it in mind."

"Your mentioning the car reminds me," said Sarah. "That was one of the things they liked best to shout about, and the windows never rattled so loud as when they were in the middle of some argument over him teaching her how to drive. I recall now, the very morning it happened they were screaming their heads off at each other over some little thing she couldn't seem to learn, or at least that was what he said."

"And what was it she couldn't learn, do you remember?" said Sergeant Rourke, walking toward the door.

"Why, it seems to me—yes, it started when he said anybody who thought she was as good a driver as she thought she was, ought to be able to remember to put the hand brake on *once* in awhile when she parked the car."

Parisian Shave
by Mark Twain

From earliest infancy it had been a cherished ambition of mine to be shaved some day in a palatial barber-shop of Paris. I wished to recline at full length in a cushioned invalid chair, with pictures about me, and sumptuous furniture; with frescoed walls and gilded arches above me, and vistas of Corinthian columns stretching far before me; with perfumes of Araby to intoxicate my senses, and the slumberous drone of distant noises to soothe me to sleep. At the end of an hour I would wake up regretfully and find my face as smooth and as soft as an infant's. Departing, I would lift my hands above that barber's head and say "Heaven bless you, my son!"

So we searched high and low, for a matter of two hours, but never a barber-shop could we see. We saw only wig-making establishments, with shocks of dead and repulsive hair bound upon the heads of painted waxen brigands who stared out from the glass boxes upon the passer-by, with their stony eyes, and scared him with the ghostly white of their countenances. We shunned these signs for a time, but finally we concluded that the wig-makers must of necessity be the barbers as well, since we could find no single legitimate representative of the fraternity. We entered and asked, and found that it was even so.

I said I wanted to be shaved. The barber inquired where my room was. I said, never mind where my room was, I wanted to be shaved—there, on the spot. The doctor said he would be shaved also. Then there was excitement among those two barbers! There was a wild consultation, and afterwards a hurrying to and fro and a feverish gathering up of razors from obscure places and a ransacking for soap. Next they took us into a little, mean, shabby back room; they got two ordinary sitting-room chairs and placed us in them, with our coats on. My old, old dream of bliss vanished into thin air!

I sat bolt upright, silent, sad and solemn. One of the wig-making villains lathered my face for ten terrible minutes and finished by plastering a mass of suds into my mouth. I expelled the nasty stuff with a strong English expletive and said, "Foreigner, beware!" Then this outlaw strapped his razor on his boot, hovered over me ominously for six fearful seconds, and then swooped down upon me like the genius of destruction. The first rake of his razor loosened the very hide from my face and lifted me out of the chair. I stormed and raved, and the other boys enjoyed it. Their beards are not strong and thick. Let us draw the curtain over this harrowing scene. Suffice it that I submitted, and went through with the cruel infliction of a shave by a French barber; tears of exquisite agony coursed down my cheeks, now and then, but I survived. Then the incipient assassin held a basin of water under my chin and slopped its contents over my face, and onto my bosom, and down the back of my neck, with a mean pretense of washing away the soap and blood. He dried my features with a towel, and was going to comb my hair; but I asked to be excused. I said, with withering irony, that it was sufficient to be skinned—I declined to be scalped.

I went away from there with my handkerchief about my face, and never, never, never desired to dream of palatial Parisian barber-shops any more. The truth is, as I believe I have since found out, that they have no barber-shops worthy of the name, in Paris—and no barbers, either, for that matter. The imposter who does duty as a barber brings his pans and napkins and implements of torture to your residence and deliberately skins you in your private apartments. Ah, I have suffered, suffered, suffered, here in Paris, but never mind—the time is coming when I shall have a dark and bloody revenge. Some day a Parisian barber will come to my room to skin me, and from that day forth, that barber will never be heard of more.

Somebody in My Bed
by James Aswell

As I continued, the Captain's interest in my story mounted. His eyes bulged as I recounted how, when I returned to my room at the tavern, through some mistake a strange girl had been given my room and was soundly asleep on what should have been my bed.

"I gazed at her," said I, "and I had never witnessed anything more beautiful. From underneath a little night cap, rivalling the snow in whiteness, fell a stray ringlet over a neck and shoulders of alabaster."

"Well?" said the Captain, giving his chair a hitch.

"Never did I look upon a bosom more perfectly formed. I took hold of the coverlet and softly pulled it down."

"Well!" said the Captain, betraying excitement.

"To her waist—" said I.

"Well!" said the Captain, dropping his newspaper.

"She had on a nightdress, buttoned up before—but softly I opened the first two buttons."

"Well!!" said the Captain, wrought to the highest pitch.

"Then," said I, "Ye gods! What a sight to gaze upon! Words fail! Just then-"

"WELL!!!" said the Captain, hitching his chair right and left, and squirting his tobacco juice against the stove so that it fairly sizzled.

"Then," I said, "I thought I was taking mean advantage of her, so I went and slept in another room."

"*It's a lie!*" shouted the Captain, jumping up and kicking over his chair. "IT'S A LIE!"

Kindly Dig Your Grave
by Stanley Ellin

The story of Madame Lagrue, the most infamously successful dealer in bad art on Butte-Montmartre, and of O'Toole, the undernourished painter, and of Fatima, the vengeful model who loved O'Toole, and of what happened to them, properly begins in Madame Lagrue's gallery on Rue Hyacinthe.

It is possible that the worst art in the whole world was displayed on the walls of the Galerie Lagrue.

Madame, of course, did not know this, nor, one must surmise, did her customers. To Madame, every picture on her walls—from the leaden landscapes to the tropical moonlights painted on black velvet, from the cunning kittens peeping out of boots to the endless array of circus clowns, some with teardrops conspicuously gleaming on their cheeks to indicate the breaking hearts beneath the painted smiles—every one of these was beautiful.

That was the first reason for her fantastic success as a dealer in low-priced art—her abominable taste.

The second reason was that long before any of her competitors, Madame Lagrue had smelled out the renaissance in faraway America. After the war, all over that golden land, it seemed, the middle-aged middle class had developed a furious appetite for, as Madame's brochure so neatly describe it, *genuine works of art, handpainted on high quality canvas by great French artists for reasonable prices.*

So, when the trickle of American interior decorators and department-store buyers became a tide regularly lapping at the summit of Butte-Montmartre, Madame was ready for it. Before her competitors around the Place du Tertre in the shadow of Sacré-Coeur knew what was happening, she had cornered the fattest part of the market, and where others occasionally sold a picture to a passing tourist, she sold pictures by the dozen and by the gross to a wholesale clientele.

Then, having created a sellers' market among those who produced the kittens and clowns, Madame saw to it that she was not made the victim of any economic law dictating that she pay higher prices for this merchandise.

Here, her true talent as an art dealer emerged most brilliantly.

Most of the artists she dealt with were a shabby, spiritless lot of hacks, and, as Madame contentedly observed, their only pressing need was for a little cash in hand every day. Not enough to corrupt them, of course, but barely enough for rent, food, and drink and the materials necessary for creating their pictures.

So where Madame's competitors, lacking her wealth, offered only dreams of glory—they would price your picture for 100 francs and give you half of that if it sold—Madame offered the reality of 20 or 30 francs cash in hand. Or, perhaps, only 10 francs. But it was cash paid on the spot, and it readily bought her first claim on the services of the painters who supplied her stock in trade.

The danger was that since Madame needed the painters as much as the painters needed Madame, it put them in a good bargaining position. It was to solve this problem that she invented a method of dealing with her stable which would have made Torquemada shake his head in admiration.

The painter, work in hand, was required to present himself at her office, a dank and frigid cubby-hole behind the showroom with barely enough room in it for an ancient rolltop desk and swivel chair and an easel on which the painting was placed for Madame's inspection. Madame, hat firmly planted on her head as if to assert her femininity—the hat was like a large black flowerpot worn upside down with a spray of dusty flowers projecting from its crown—would sit like an empress in the swivel chair and study the painting with an expression of distaste, her eyes narrowing and lips compressing as she examined its details. Then, on a piece of scrap paper, carefully shielding the paper with her other hand to conceal it, she would jot down a figure.

That was the price the artist had to meet. If he asked a single franc more than the figure on that scrap of paper, he would be turned away on the spot. There was no second chance offered, no opportunity to bargain. He might have started out from his hutch on Rue Norvins confident that the property under his arm was worth at least 50 francs this time. Before he was halfway to Rue Hyacinthe, the confidence would have dwindled, the asking price fallen to 40 francs or even 30 as the image of Madame Lagrue's craggy features rose before him. By the time he had propped his picture on the easel he was willing to settle for 20 and praying that the figure she was mysteriously noting on her scrap paper wasn't 10.

"*A vous la balle,*" Madame would say, meaning it was his turn to get into the game. "How much?"

Thirty, the painter would think desperately. Every leaf on those trees is painted to perfection. You can almost hear the water of that brook gurgling. This one is worth at least 30. But that sour look on the old miser's face. Maybe she's in no mood for brooks and trees this morning—

"Twenty?" he would say faintly, the sweat cold on his brow.

Madame would hold up the scrap of paper before him to read for himself, and whatever he read there would fill him with helpless rage. If he had asked too little, he could only curse his lack of courage. If too much, it meant no sale, and there was no use raising a hubbub about it. Madame did not tolerate hubbubs, and since she had the massive frame and short temper of a Norman farm hand, one respected her sensibilities in such matters.

No, all one could do was take a rejected picture to Florelle, the dealer down the block, and offer it to him for sale at commission, which meant waiting a long time or forever for any return on it. Or, if Madame bought the picture, take the pittance she offered and head directly to the Café Hyacinthe next door for a few quick ones calculated to settle the nerves. Next to Madame Lagrue herself, it was the Café Hyacinthe that profited most from her method of dealing with her painters.

A vous la balle. It was a bitter jest among the painters in Madame's stable, a greeting they sometimes used acidly on one another, the croaking of a bird of ill omen which nightmarishly entered their dreams and could only be muted by the happy thought of someday landing a fist on Madame's bulbous nose.

Of them all, the one who was worst treated by Madame and yet seemed to suffer least under her oppression was O'Toole, the American painter who had drifted to Butte-Montmartre long ago in pursuit of his art. He was at least as shabby and unkempt and undernourished as the others, but he lived with a perpetual, gentle smile of intoxication on his lips, sustained by his love of painting and by the cheapest *marc* the Café Hyacinthe could provide.

Marc is distilled from the grape pulp left in the barrel after the wine is pressed, and when the wine happens to be a Romanée-

Conti of a good year, its *marc* makes an excellent drink. The Café Hyacinthe's *marc*, on the other hand, was carelessly, sometimes surreptitiously, distilled from the pulp of unripe grapes going to make the cheapest *vin du pays*, and it had the taste and impact of grape-flavored gasoline.

As far as anyone could tell, it provided all the sustenance O'Toole required, all the vision he needed to paint an endless succession of pastoral scenes in the mode of the Barbizon School. The ingredients of each scene were the same—a pond, a flowery glen, a small stand of birch trees; but O'Toole varied their arrangement, sometimes putting the trees on one side of the pond, sometimes on the other. The warmth of a bottle of marc in his belly, the feel of the brush in his hand, this was all the bliss O'Toole asked for.

He had a hard time of it before entering Madame's stable. During the tourist season each year he had worked at a stand near the Place du Tertre doing quick portraits in charcoal—*Likeness Guaranteed or Your Money Back;* but business was never good since, although the likenesses were indisputable, naive and kindly mirror images, the portraits were wholly uninspired. His heart just wasn't in them. Trees and flowery glens and ponds, that was where his heart lay. The discovery that Madame Lagrue was willing to put money in his hand for them was the great discovery of his life. He was her happiest discovery, too. Those pastorals, she soon learned, were much in demand by the Americans. They sold as fast as she could put them on display.

O'Toole was early broken in to Madame's method of doing business. That first terrible experience when he was taught there was no retreat from his overestimate of a picture's value, no chance to quote a second price, so that he had to trudge away, pastoral under his arm unsold, had been enough to break his spirit completely. After that, all he asked was 20 francs for a large picture and 10 for a small one and so established almost a happy relationship with Madame.

The one break in the relationship had been when Florelle, who owned the shop on the other side of the Café Hyacinthe and who was not a bad sort for an art dealer, had finally persuaded him to hand over one of his paintings for sale at commission. The next time O'Toole went to do business with Madame Lagrue he was dismayed to find her regarding him with outright loathing.

"No sale," she said shortly. "No business. I'm not interested."

O'Toole foggily stared at his picture on the easel, trying to understand what was wrong with it.

"But it's beautiful," he said. "Look at it. Look at those flowers. It took me three days just to do those flowers."

"You're breaking my heart," said Madame. "Ingrate. Traitor. You have another dealer now. Let him buy your obscene flowers."

In the end, O'Toole had to reclaim his picture from Florelle and beg Madame's forgiveness, almost with tears in his eyes. And Madame, contemplating the flow of landscapes which would be coming her way until O'Toole drank himself to death, almost had tears of emotion in her own eyes. The landscapes were bringing her at least 100 francs each, and the thought of 500 to 1000 percent profit on a picture can make any art dealer emotional.

Then Fatima entered the scene.

Fatima was not her name, of course; it was what some wag at the Café Hyacinthe had christened her when she had started to hang around there between sessions of modeling for life classes. She was a small, swarthy Algerian, very plain of feature, but with magnificent, dark, velvety eyes, coal-black hair which hung in a tangle to her waist, and a lush figure. She was also known to have the worst disposition of anyone who frequented the café and, with a few drinks in her, the foulest mouth.

"She's not even eighteen yet," the bartender once observed, listening awestruck as she told off a hapless painter who had sat down uninvited at her table. "Think how she'll sound when she's a full-grown woman!"

She also had her sentimental side, blubbering unashamedly at sad scenes in the movies, especially those in which lovers were parted or children abused, and had a way of carting stray kittens back to her room on the Rue des Saulles until her concierge, no sentimentalist at all, raised a howl about it.

So although it was unexpected, it was not totally mystifying to the patrons of the Café Hyacinthe that Fatima should suddenly demonstrate an interest in O'Toole one rainy day when he stumbled into the café and stood in the doorway dripping cold rainwater on the floor, sneezing his head off, and, no question about it, looking even more forlorn than any of the stray kittens Fatima's concierge objected to.

Fatima was alone at her usual table, sullenly nursing her second Pernod. Her eyes fell on O'Toole, taking him in from head to foot, and a light of interest dawned in them. She crooked a finger.

"Hey, you. Come over here."

It was the first time she had ever invited anyone to her table. O'Toole glanced over his shoulder to see whom she was delivering the invitation to and then pointed to himself.

"Me?"

"Yes, you, stupid. Come here and sit down."

He did. And it was Fatima who not only stood him a bottle of wine but ordered a towel from the bartender so that she could dry his sodden hair. The patrons at the other tables gaped as she toweled away, O'Toole's head bobbing back and forth helplessly under her ministrations.

"You're a real case, aren't you?" she told O'Toole. "Don't you have brains enough to wear a hat in the rain so you don't go around trying to kill yourself in this stinking weather?"

"A hat?" O'Toole said vaguely.

"Yes, imbecile. That thing one uses to keep his head dry in the rain."

"Oh," said O'Toole. Then he said in timid apology, "I don't have one."

Everyone in the café watched with stupefaction as Fatima tenderly patted his cheek.

"It's all right, baby," she said. "Someone left one in my room last week. When we get out of here you'll walk back there and I'll give it to you."

The whole thing came about as abruptly as that. And it was soon clear to the most cynical beholder that Fatima had fallen hopelessly in love with this particular stray cat. She began to bathe regularly, she combed out the tangles in her splendid black hair, she showed up at the café wearing dresses recently laundered. And, surest sign of all, the little red welts and the bite marks once bestowed on her neck and shoulders by various overnight acquaintances all faded away.

As for O'Toole, Fatima mothered him passionately. She moved him into her room, lock, stock, and easel; saw to it that he was decently fed and clothed; threatened to slit the throat of the bartender of the Café Hyacinthe if he dared serve her man any more of that poisonous *marc* instead of a drinkable wine; and promised to gut anyone in the café who made the slightest remark about her grand amour.

No one there or elsewhere on Butte-Montmartre made any remarks. In fact, with only one exception among them, they found the situation rather touching. The one exception was Madame Lagrue.

It was not merely that paintings of nudes outraged Madame—in her loudly expressed opinion, the Louvre itself would do well to burn its filthy exhibitions of nakedness—but the knowledge that the degraded models for such paintings should be allowed to walk the very streets she walked was enough to turn her stomach. And that one of these degraded, venal types should somehow take possession of a cherished property like O'Toole—!

Madame recognized that the corruption had set in the day O'Toole appeared before her almost unrecognizably dandified. The shabby old suit was the same, but it had been cleaned and patched. The shoes were still scuffed and torn, but the knotted pieces of string in them had been replaced by shoelaces. The cheeks were shaven for the first time in memory, and, to Madame's narrowed eyes, they did not appear quite so hollow as they used to be. All in all, here was the sad spectacle of a once dedicated artist being prettified and fattened up like a shoat for the market, and, no doubt, having the poison of avarice injected into him by the slut who was doing all this prettifying and fattening. It was easy to visualize the way Fatima must be demanding of him that he ask some preposterous price for his landscape on the easel. Well, Madame grimly decided, if a showdown had to come, it might as well come right now.

Madame glanced at the landscape and at O'Toole, who stood there beaming with admiration at it, then wrote down on her scrap of paper the usual price of 20 francs.

"Come on," she said tartly, "*A vous la balle*. Name your price. I'm a busy woman. I don't have all day for this nonsense."

O'Toole stopped beaming. Just before departing for the gallery he had been admonished by Fatima to demand 100 francs for this painting.

"Simpleton," she had said kindly, "you've put a week's work into this thing. Florelle told me a painting like this was worth at least a hundred francs to the old witch. You have to stop letting her bleed you to death. This time if she offers only twenty or thirty, just spit in her ugly face."

"Yes, this time," O'Toole had said bravely.

Now, with Madame's flinty eyes on him, he smiled not so bravely. He opened his mouth to speak, closed it, opened it again.

"Well?" said Madame in a voice of doom.

"Would twenty francs be all right?" said O'Toole.

"Yes," said Madame triumphantly.

It was the first of her many triumphs over Fatima's baleful influence. The greatest triumph, one Madame herself never even knew of, came the time Fatima announced to O'Toole that she would accompany him on his next sales meeting. If he didn't have the guts of a decayed flounder in dealing with this exploiter, at least she, thank God, did. She watched as O'Toole, after giving her a long, troubled look, started to pack his paints together.

"What are you doing, numskull?" she demanded.

"I'm leaving," O'Toole said with a dignity that astonished and alarmed her. "This is no good. A woman shouldn't mix in her husband's business."

"What husband? We're not married, imbecile."

"We're not?"

"No, we're not."

"I'm leaving anyhow," said O'Toole, somewhat confusingly. "I don't want anyone to help me sell my paintings."

It took Fatima a flood of tears and two bottles of vin rouge to wheedle him out of his decision, and she never made the same mistake again. It was a lost cause, she saw. All O'Toole wanted besides the pleasure of painting was the pleasure of having a ready cash market for his paintings, and Madame Lagrue, by offering him one, had bought his soul like the devil.

Until she had to face this realization Fatima had merely detested Madame Lagrue. Now she hated her with a devouring hatred. Oh, to have revenge on the vile old woman, some lovely revenge that would make her scream her head off. Many a night after that Fatima happily put herself to sleep with thoughts of revenge circling through her head, most of them having to do with hot irons, and would wake in the morning knowing despondently how futile those happy thoughts were.

Then Nature decided to play a card.

O'Toole was, as is so often the case, one of the last to learn the news. He received it with honest bewilderment.

"You're going to have a baby?" he said, trying to understand.

"We are going to have a baby," Fatima corrected. "Both of us. It's already on the way. Is that clear?"

"Yes, of course," said O'Toole with becoming sobriety. "A baby."

"That's right. And it means some big changes around here. For one thing, it means we really are getting married now, because my kid's not going to be any miserable, fatherless alley rat. It's going to have a nice little mama and papa, and a nice little house to grow up in. You're not already married, are you?"

"No."

"Well, I'll take my chances on that. And for another thing, we're getting out of Paris. I've had my bellyful of this horrible place, and so have you. We're packing up and going to my home town in Algeria. To Bougie, where the kid will get some sunshine. My aunt and uncle own a café there, a nice little place, and they've got no kids of their own, so they'd give anything to have me help them run the joint. You can paint meanwhile."

"A baby," said O'Toole. To Fatima's immense relief he seemed to be rather pleased with the idea. Then his face darkened. "Bougie," he said. "But how will I sell my paintings?"

"You can ship them to your old witch. You think she'll turn down such bargains because they come in the mail?"

O'Toole considered this unhappily. "I'll have to talk to her about it."

"No, I will, whether you like it or not," said Fatima, risking everything on this throw of the dice. "I've got another piece of business to settle with her anyhow."

"What business?"

"Money. We'll need plenty of it to get to Bougie and set up in a house there. And it wouldn't hurt to have a few francs extra put away for the bad times so the kid can always have a pair of shoes when he needs them."

"He?"

"Or she. It's even more expensive with a girl, if it comes to that. Or would you rather have your daughter selling her innocent little body as soon as she's able to walk?"

O'Toole shook his head vigorously at the suggestion. Then he looked wonderingly at the mother-to-be.

"But this money—" he said. "You think Madame Lagrue will give it to us?"

"Yes."

Finally, he had found something on which he could express a firm opinion. "You're crazy," he said.

"Am I?" Fatima retorted. "Well, simpleton, you leave it to me and I'll show you how crazy I am. And get this straight. If you don't let me handle that miserable old hyena my own way, I'll turn you over to the cops for giving me a baby without marrying me, and they'll throw you in jail for twenty years. Nobody does any painting in jail either. He just sits there and rots until he's an old man. Do you understand?"

For the first time O'Toole found himself face to face with a presence even more overwhelming than Madame Lagrue's.

"Yes," he said.

"All right then," said Fatima. "Now get a nice big canvas ready. You're going to paint me a picture."

So it was that a week later, Fatima appeared in the Galerie Lagrue bearing a large painting clumsily wrapped in newspaper. Madame's assistant, a pale, timid girl, tried to bar her from the office and was shoved aside.

Madame was at her desk in the office. At the sight of her visitor, who came bearing what must be an original O'Toole, she quivered with indignation. She aimed a commanding forefinger at the door.

"Out!" she said. "Out! I don't do business with your kind!"

Fatima summed up her answer to this in a single unprintable word. She slammed the office door shut with a backward kick of the foot, hoisted the painting to the easel, and stripped its wrapping from it.

"Is it your business to refuse masterpieces, harpy?" she demanded. "Look at this."

Madame Lagrue looked. Then she looked again, her eyes opening wide in horror.

This painting was larger than any O'Toole had ever offered her before, and it was not the usual landscape. No, this time it was a nude. A ripely curved, full-blown nude with not an inch of her fleshy body left to the imagination. And with Fatima in a tight, highly revealing blouse and skirt standing side by side with the painting, there was no doubt in Madame's shocked mind as to who its model had been. The nude was an uninspired pink and white, not swarthy as Fatima was, but it was without question Fatima's body so painstakingly delineated on the canvas.

But that was only the beginning of the horror, because while it was Fatima from the neck down, it was, abomination of abominations, Madame Lagrue herself from the neck up. Photographically exact, glassy-eyed, the black flowerpot upside down on the head with the dusty flowers sprouting from it crown, the stern face staring at Madame was Madame's own face.

"A masterpiece, eh?" said Fatima sweetly.

Madame made a strangled noise in her throat, then found her voice. "What an insult! What an outrage!"

She came to her feet prepared to rend the outrage to shreds, and suddenly there was a wicked little paring knife gleaming in Fatima's hand. Madame hastily sat down again.

"That's better," Fatima advised her. "Lay one little finger on this picture before you buy it, you old sow, and I'll slice your nose off."

"Buy it?" Madame refused to believe her ears. "Do you really believe I'd buy an obscenity like that?"

"Yes. Because if you don't, Florelle will take it on commission. And he'll be glad to put it right in the middle of his window where everyone on Butte-Montmartre can see it. Then everyone in Paris. Those fancy Americans you do business with will see it, too. They'll all have a chance to see it, bloodsucker, because I'll tell Florelle not to sell it at any price for at least a year. It'll be worth it to him to keep in his window just to draw trade. Think that over. Think it over very carefully. I'm in no rush."

Madame thought it over very carefully for a long time.

"It's blackmail," she said at last in bitter resignation. "Plain blackmail. A shakedown, nothing more or less."

"You've hit the nail right on the head," Fatima said cheerfully.

"What if I submit to this blackmail?" Madame asked warily. "Can I do whatever I wish with this disgusting object?"

"Anything. If you pay its price."

"And what is its price?"

Fatima reached into a pocket and came up with a folded slip of paper which she waved tantalizingly just out of Madame's reach.

"The price is written down here, old lady. Now all you have to do is meet it, and the picture is yours. But remember this. Offer me one solitary franc less than what's written down on this paper, and the deal is off. There's no second chance. You get one turn in this game, that's all. Prove yourself one franc too thrifty, and the picture goes straight to Florelle."

"What kind of talk is that?" Madame demanded angrily. "A game, she says. I'm willing to do business with this creature, and she talks about games."

"Vulture," retorted Fatima. "Destroyer of helpless artists. Don't you think everyone knows this is the way you do business? *A vous la balle*, eh? Kindly dig your grave, artist, and bury yourself. Isn't that the way it goes? Well, now it's your turn to learn how it feels."

Madame opened her arms wide in piteous appeal. "But how can I possibly know what you intend to rob me of? How can I even guess what it would cost to buy you off?"

"True," admitted Fatima. "Well, I'm softhearted so I'll give you a hint. My man and I are moving to Bougie in Algeria, and we'll need travel money for that. And some decent clothes and a trunk to put them in. And we want to buy a little house there—"

"A house!" said Madame, the blood draining from her face.

"A little house. Nothing much, but it must have electricity. And a motor bicycle to get around on."

Madame Lagrue clasped her hands tightly against her stout bosom and rocked back and forth in the chair. She looked at the nude on the easel and hastily averted her eyes from it.

"Dear God," she whimpered, "What have I done to deserve such treatment?"

"And," said Fatima relentlessly, "a little pourboire, a little money extra to put in the bank like respectable people should. That's what I see in my future, old lady. You've got a good head on your shoulders, so you shouldn't have much trouble adding it all up." She held up the slip of paper. "But make sure your arithmetic is right. Remember, you only get one chance to guess what's written here."

In her rage and frustration Madame found herself groping wildly for elusive figures. Travel money to Algeria, 300 francs. No, 400. No, better make it 500, because rather safe than sorry. Another 500 should certainly buy all the clothes needed for such a pair of ragamuffins. Throw in 100 for the trunk. But a house, even a mud hut, with electricity! Madame groaned aloud. What, in the devil's name, would that cost? Possibly 7000 or 8000 francs. And pourboire, the slut had said, and a motor bicycle. There was no use trying to work it all out to the exact franc. The best thing to do was call it a round 10,000.

Ten thousand francs! Madame Lagrue felt as if a cold wind were howling around her, as if she were being buried alive beneath a snowdrift of misery.

"Well?" said Fatima cruelly. "Let's have it. *A vous la balle, madame.*"

"I'll have the law on you," croaked Madame Lagrue. I'll have the police destroy that scandalous object."

"Save your breath, miser. This is a work of art, and you know as well as I do that nobody destroys a work of art because it might bother someone. Now enough of such nonsense. What's your offer?"

Madame stared at the slip of paper in her tormentor's hand. Oh, for one little look at the figure written on it—

"Ten thousand," she gasped.

The look of contempt on Fatima's face, the curl of that lip, told Madame she had miscalculated after all, she had cut it too fine. She thought of the crowds gathered before Florelle's window staring with obscene delight at the picture; she thought of them gathering before her own window, leering and nudging each other, hoping to get a glimpse of her in her disgrace. She'd never be able to go out on the street again. She'd be driven out of business in a month, a week—

"No, wait!" she cried. "I meant fifteen thousand! Of course, fifteen thousand. I don't know what got into me. It was a slip of the tongue!"

"You said ten thousand."

"I swear it was a mistake! Take fifteen. I insist you take it."

Fatima glanced at her slip of paper. She gnawed her lip, weighing the case in her mind. "All right, I'll be merciful. But I want my money right now."

"I don't have that much in cash here. I'll send the girl to the bank."

"And I want a paper to show that the deal is strictly on the level."

"Yes, of course. I'll make it out for you while we're waiting."

The pale, timid assistant must have run like a rabbit. She was back in almost no time with an envelope stuffed full of banknotes which she handed to Madame Lagrue through the partly opened door of the office. Tears trickled down Madame's cheeks as she gave the money to Fatima.

"This is my life's blood," Madame said. "You've drained me dry, criminal."

"Liar, you've made a million from your poor painters," Fatima retorted. "It's time at least one of them was paid what you owe him."

As she left, she crumpled the slip of paper in her hand and carelessly tossed it to the floor.

"You don't have to see us off at the plane," she said in farewell. "Just stay here and enjoy your picture."

No sooner had the office door slammed behind her than Madame snatched up the crumpled paper from the floor and opened it with trembling fingers. Her eyes, as she saw the figure written on it in a large childish hand, almost bulged from her head.

Twenty francs!

GAMBLING
by Ron Fawcett

Scene: The Salon, Windemere Club, off Berkeley Square, London

"Willie" Pierce and "Bunty" Blore were having sherry at the bar. They were silent for a bit, then Pierce said, "I say, Bunty."

"Mmh?"

"Heard about Kit Cranmere?"

"No."

Pierce sipped his sherry. "Won a packet at Cockford's last night."

"A packet?"

"Right. Ten thousand pounds."

"Good Lord, Willie. Are you shaw?!" Blore sipped his sherry.

"Quite. Ah, here comes Ilford. Hullo, Colly. I say, Bunty and I were talking about Kit Cranmere. They say he won ten thousand quid at Cockford's last night."

Ilford raised his glass of ale. "Cheers." He drank.

"Heard anything about that, Colly?" asked Blore.

"Mmh," said Ilford. "Saw it with my own eyes, Bunty."

"Ah, then—" crowed Pierce.

"But it wasn't Kit Cranmere, Willie; it was his brother Ainsly. And it wasn't at Cockford's, it was at the Curzon. And 'twasn't ten thousand quid. It was six. And he didn't win it, old man, he lost it." Ilford took a deep swig. "In all other respects, old boy, your account is entirely correct."

Fenimore Cooper's Literary Offenses
by Mark Twain

I was a freshman in college when somewhere I read how Goethe plowed into Kant's Critique of Pure Reason *but had to quit it after the first chapter because he thought he'd go insane. I couldn't appreciate this statement till, later that semester, I was assigned James Fenimore Cooper's* The Deerslayer *in my English Lit class. I only got about 4,000 pages into it and decided to switch over to the* Cliff Notes; *but the college bookstore was sold out. I finally begged a used copy off a sophomore, and noticed the primer was on its 7,934th printing. For twenty years I remained convinced than no living man had actually read* The Deerslayer, *cover to cover. Then, my friend Paul Edwards referred me to Mark Twain's* Fenimore Cooper's Literary Offenses, *and I realized that the Father of American Letters had actually read not only* The Deerslayer, *but* The Pathfinder *as well. Twain had problems with both texts. Here is some of what Twain said:*

The Pathfinder and The Deerslayer stand at the head of Cooper's novels as artistic creations. There are others of his works which contain parts as perfect as are to be found in these, and scenes even more thrilling. Not one can be compared with either of them as a finished whole.

"The defects in both of these tales are comparatively slight. They were pure works of art." —*Prof. Lounsbury.*

"The five tales reveal an extraordinary fullness of invention . . . One of the very greatest characters in fiction, Natty Bumppo . . . The craft of the woodsman, the tricks of the trapper, all the delicate art of the forest, were familiar to Cooper from his youth up." —*Prof. Brander Matthews.*

"Cooper is the greatest artist in the domain of romantic fiction yet produced by America." —*Wilkie Collins.*

It seems to me that it was far from right for the Professor of English Literature in Yale, the Professor of English Literature in

Columbia, and Wilkie Collins to deliver opinions on Cooper's literature without having read some of it. It would have been much more decorous to keep silent and let persons talk who have read Cooper.

Cooper's art has some defects. In one place in *Deerslayer*, and in the restricted space of two-thirds of a page, Cooper has scored 114 offenses against literary art, out of a possible 115. It breaks the record.

There are nineteen rules governing literary art in the domain of romantic fiction—some say twenty-two. In *Deerslayer* Cooper violated eighteen of them. These eighteen require:

1. That a tale shall accomplish something and arrive somewhere. But the *Deerslayer* tale accomplishes nothing and arrives in the air.

2. They require that the episodes of a tale shall be necessary parts of the tale, and shall help to develop it. But as the *Deerslayer* tale is not a tale, and accomplishes nothing and arrives nowhere, the episodes have no rightful place in the work, since there was nothing for them to develop.

3. They require that the personages in a tale shall be alive, except in the case of corpses, and that always the reader shall be able to tell the corpses from the others. But this detail has often been overlooked in the *Deerslayer* tale.

4. They require that the personages in a tale, both dead and alive, shall exhibit a sufficient excuse for being there. But, this detail also has been overlooked in the *Deerslayer* tale.

5. They require that when the personages in a tale deal in conversation, the talk shall sound like human talk, and be talk such as human beings would be likely to talk in the given circumstances, and have a discoverable meaning, also a discoverable purpose, and a show of relevancy, and remain in the neighborhood of the subject in hand, and be interesting to the reader, and help out the tale, and stop when the people cannot think of anything more to say. But this requirement has been ignored from the beginning of the *Deerslayer* tale to the end of it.

6. They require that when the author describes the character of a personage in his tale, the conduct and conversation of that personage shall justify said description. But this law gets little or no attention in the *Deerslayer* tale, as Natty Bumppo's case will amply prove.

7. They require that when a personage talks like an illustrated, gilt-edged, tree-calk, hand-tooled, seven-dollar Friendship's Offering in the beginning of a paragraph, he shall not talk like a negro minstrel in the end of it. But this rule is flung down and danced upon in the *Deerslayer* tale.

8. They require that crass stupidities shall not be played upon the reader as "the craft of the woodsman, the delicate art of the forest," by either the author or the people in the tale. But this rule is persistently violated in the *Deerslayer* tale.

9. They require that the personages in a tale shall confine themselves to possibilities and let miracles alone; or, if they venture a miracle, the author must so plausibly set it forth as to make it look possible and reasonable. But these rules are not respected in the *Deerslayer* tale.

10. They require that the author shall make the reader feel a deep interest in the personages of his tale and in their fate; and that he shall make the reader love the good people in the tale and hate the bad ones. But the reader of the *Deerslayer* tale dislikes the good people in it, is indifferent to others, and wishes they would all get drowned together.

11. They require that the characters in a tale shall be so clearly defined that the reader can tell beforehand what each will do in a given emergency. But in the *Deerslayer* tale this rule is vacated.

In addition to these large rules there are some little ones. These require that the author shall:

12. *Say* what he is proposing to say, not merely come near it.
13. Use the right word, not its second cousin.
14. Eschew surplusage.
15. Not omit necessary details.
16. Avoid slovenliness of form.
17. Use good grammar.
18. Employ a simple and straightforward style.

Even these seven are coldly and persistently violated in the *Deerslayer* tale.

Cooper's gift in the way of invention was not a rich endowment; but such as it was he liked to work it, he was pleased with the effects, and indeed he did some sweet things with it. In his little box of stage properties he kept six or eight cunning devices, tricks, artifices for his savages and woodsmen to deceive and circumvent each other with, and he was never so happy as when he was working these innocent things and seeing them go. A favorite one was to make a moccasined person tread in the tracks of the moccasined enemy, and thus hide his own trail. Cooper wore out barrels and barrels of moccasins in working that trick. Another stage property that he pulled out of his box pretty frequently was his broken twig. He prized his broken twig above all the rest of his effects, and worked it the hardest. It is a restful chapter in any book of his when somebody doesn't step on a dry twig and alarm all the reds and whites for two hundred yards around. Every time a Cooper person is in peril, and absolute silence is worth four dollars a minute, he is sure to step on a dry twig. There may be a hundred handier things to step on, but that wouldn't satisfy Cooper.

So What?

A father was berating his son who was reluctant to do his homework. "When Abraham Lincoln was your age," the father lectured, "he walked ten miles to school each day and then studied by the light of the fire in his log cabin."

"So what?" the boy rejoined. "When John Kennedy was your age, he was president."

The Road to Miltown
by S.J. Perelman

SCENE: *A one-room apartment in Manhattan occupied by April Monkhood, a young career woman. At some time prior to rise, April and her four walls have tired of each other, and she has called in Fussfeld, a neighborhood decorator, to give the premises the twenty-five transfusions recommended above. Fussfeld, a lineal descendant of Brigadier General Sir Harvey Fussfeld-Gorgas, the genius who pacified the Sudan, has attacked the assignment with the same zeal that characterized his famous relative. He has placed at stage center a magnificent specimen of Bechtel's flowering crab, the boughs of which are so massive that it has been necessary to stay them with cables and turnbuckles. This has perforce complicated the problem of the fish-net partitions on their ceiling tracks, but, fortunately, most of these have ripped off and now descend from the branches, supplying a romantic effect akin to that of Spanish moss. What with the hodgepodge of damask, yard goods, fake leopard skin, floral wallpaper, silk fringe, and notary seals, it is difficult at first to distinguish any animate object. Finally, though, the eye picks out a rather scrawny kitten, licking its lips by an overturned goldfish bowl. A moment later, April Monkhood enters from the kitchenette, practically on all fours. She is a vivacious brownette in knee-hugging poltroons, with a retroussé nose which she wears in a horsetail. Behind her comes Fussfeld, a small, haggard gentleman with a monocle he affects for chic. However, since he is constantly losing it in the décor and scrabbling about for it, he fails to achieve any impressive degree of sang-froid.*

FUSSFELD (*dubiously*): I'm not so sure it's advisable, dusting spangles over the gas stove like that. The pilot light—

APRIL: Now, Mr. Feldpot, don't be an old fuss—I mean stop worrying, will you? It's gay, it's chintzy. It's a whiff of Mardi Gras and the storied Vieux Carré of New Orleans.

FUSSFELD (*with a shrug*): Listen, if you want to run down a fire escape in your nightgown, that's your privilege. (*Looking around*) Well, does the job suit you O.K.?

APRIL: Mad about it, my dear—simply transported. Of course, it doesn't quite have a feeling of being lived in . . .

FUSSFELD: I'd sprinkle around a few periodicals, or a can of salted peanuts or so. Anyway, a place gets more homey after your friends drop around.

APRIL: Golly, I can't wait to have my housewarming. Can you imagine when people step off the dumbwaiter and see this room by candlelight?

FUSSFELD (*faintly*): You—er—you're hoisting them up here?

APRIL: How else? We'll be using the stairs outside to eat on.

FUSSFELD: M-m-m. I'm trying to visualize it.

APRIL: I thought of Basque place-mats, two on each stair, and sweet little favors made of putty. Don't you think that would be amusing?

FUSSFELD: Oh, great, great. (*Produces a statement.*) I got everything itemized here except what you owe the paper-hanger. When he gets out of Bloomingdale, he'll send you a separate bill.

APRIL (*frowning*): Sixteen hundred and ninety-three dollars. Frankly, it's a bit more than I expected.

FUSSFELD: Well, after all, you can't pick up this kind of stuff for a song. Those notary seals, for instance. We used nine dozen at fifty cents apiece. The guy at the stationery store had to witness each one.

APRIL: I know, but you list four hundred dollars for structural work.

FUSSFELD: We had to raise the ceiling to squeeze in the tree. The plumber was here three days changing the pipes around.

APRIL (*gaily tossing aside the bill*): Ah, well, it's only money. I'll mail you a check shortly.

FUSSFELD: No hurry—any time in the next forty-eight hours. (*Carelessly*) You still work for the same concern, don't you?

APRIL: Certainly. Why?

FUSSFELD: In case I have to garnishee your pay. (*A knock at the door. April crosses to it, admits Cyprian Voles. The associate editor of a phar-*

maceutical trade journal, he is a rabbity, diffident young man with vague literary aspirations. He is at present compiling The Pleasures of Shag, *an anthology of essays relative to smoking, which will contain excerpts from Barrie's* My Lady Nicotine, *Machen's* The Anatomy of Tobacco, *etc., and which will be remaindered within thirty days of publication.*)

CYPRIAN: Am I too early? You said six-thirty.

APRIL: Of course not, dear. Cyprian, this is my decorative-relations counsel, Mr. Fussfeld—Mr. Voles.

FUSSFELD: Likewise. Well, I got to be running along, Miss Monkhood. About that check—

APRIL: Just as soon as my ship comes in.

FUSSFELD: I'll be studying the maritime news. (*Exits. Cyprian, meanwhile, has backed into a mobile of fish and chips suspended overhead and is desperately fighting to disengage it from his hat.*)

APRIL (*thirsting for approval*): Isn't the flat delectable? Have you ever in your whole life seen anything so cozy?

CYPRIAN: Yes, it—it's stunning. It's really you—it captures the inner essence—that is, the outer inwardness—

APRIL: You don't think it's overdone, do you?

CYPRIAN: Overdone? Why, it's stark! You couldn't omit one detail without damaging the whole composition.

APRIL (*hugging him*): You old sorcerer. You know just the words to thaw a woman's heart. Now, I've an inspiration. Instead of going out for dinner, let's have powdered snails and a bottle of Old Rabbinical under the crab.

CYPRIAN (*fingering his collar*): Er—to tell you the truth, I—I find it a little close in here. You see, I fell into a grain elevator one time when I was small—

APRIL: Nonsense, it'll be heaps of fun. I loathe those big, expensive restaurants. Sit ye doon while I mix us an apéritif. (*She thrusts him backward onto the studio couch, almost decapitating him with a guy wire, then whisks a bottle from a cabinet.*) Who do you suppose called me today? My husband, of all people.

CYPRIAN: Hanh? You never told me you were married.

APRIL: Oh, Sensualdo and I've been separated for years. He's a monster—an absolute fiend.

CYPRIAN: Is he a Mexican?

APRIL: Uh-uh—Peruvian. One of those insanely jealous types, always opening your mail and accusing you of carrying on with his friends. He tried to stab a man I was having a coke with. That's what broke up our marriage.

CYPRIAN: W—where is he now?

APRIL: Right here in New York. His lawyers are trumping up evidence for a divorce—What's the matter?

CYPRIAN (*he has risen and sways dangerously*): I feel faint . . . spots before the eyes . . .

APRIL: Lie down. I'll get you some water—

CYPRIAN (*panting*): No, no. I've got to get out of here. The walls are closing in. (*He becomes entangled in a pile of mill-end remnants and flounders hopelessly. Simultaneously, a peremptory knock at door.*)

VOICE (*offscene*): Open up there!

CYPRIAN (*in an agonized whisper*): Who's that?

APRIL: I don't know, unless—

ANOTHER VOICE (*offscene*): Open the door, you tramp, else we break eet down!

APRIL (*biting her lip*): Damnation. It's Sensualdo. (*Grabbing Cyprian's arm.*) Quick, into the bathroom—no, wait a second, stand over there! (*She snatches a handful of notary seals from a shelf, and, moistening them, begins pasting them at random on his face.*)

CYPRIAN (*struggling*): What are you doing?

APRIL: Sh-h-h, never mind—help me! Stick them on your clothes—anywhere! (*Pandemonium at the door as Sensualdo attempts to kick in the panels. April, in the meantime, has found a heavy iron ring—conveniently included in the props by the stage manager—and now arranges it to dangle from Cyprian's outstretched hand.*) There. Now lean forward and try to look like a hitching post. That's perfect—don't budge! (*She runs to the door, yanks it open. Sensualdo, an overwrought Latin in the world's most expensive vicuna coat, erupts in, flanked by two private detectives.)*

SENSUALDO *(roaring)*: Where is thees animal which he is defiling my home? *(He and his aides halt in stupefaction as they behold the apartment.)*

APRIL: Get out! How dare you barge in without a warrant? Help! Police!

FIRST SHAMUS *(ignoring her)*: Holy cow! What kind of a joint is this?

SECOND SHAMUS: It's a thrift shop. Look at that statue with a ring in its hand.

FIRST SHAMUS *(to Sensualdo)*: Hey, Bright Eyes, we didn't hire out to break in no store. I'm takin' a powder.

SENSUALDO: Eet's a trick! Search in the closets, the bathroom—

SECOND SHAMUS: And lay in the workhouse ninety days? No sirree. Come on, Havemeyer. *(The pair exit. Sensualdo, his hood engorged with venom, turns on April.)*

SENSUALDO: You leetle devil. One day you go too far.

APRIL *(tremulously)*: Oh, darling, don't—you mustn't. I'm so vulnerable when you look at me like that.

SENSUALDO *(seizing her roughly)*: Do not play pelota weeth my heart, woman. You mean you are still caring for me?

APRIL: Passionately, joyously. With every fiber of my being. Take me, hold me, fold me. *(Her eyelids capsize.)* To kiss anyone else is like a mustache without salt.

SENSUALDO: Ah-h-h, Madre de Dios, how you set my blood on fire anew. Let me take you out of all thees—to a hilltop in Cuzco, to the eternal snows of the Andes—

APRIL *(simply)*: Geography doesn't matter, sugar. With you I could be happy in a hallway. *(They depart, absorbed in each other. Cyprian holds his pose a few seconds, and then, straightening, tiptoes after them as warily as the goldfish bowl on his foot permits.)*

CURTAIN

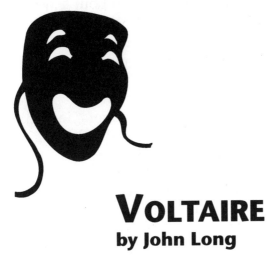

VOLTAIRE
by John Long

I went to Rancho Francaise in Madera, Mexico, on the business of my grandfather's Texas stud ranch, which Dad was trying to sell off. A Mexican rancher with the impossible name of Voltaire (whose great-great grandfather, a French embezzler and bigamist, had fled to Mexico in the 1840s), a fringe acquaintance of my grandfather, was looking to buy and wanted financial reports and all the rest. I went down to hand-deliver the papers, intending to stay three days, enough time for Voltaire to study the documents with his attorney and reach a decision I could take back to Dad. Several years before, Voltaire had argued with and finally horsewhipped Luther Pettibone at his own quarterhorse ranch in El Paso, then dashed back to Mexico. With a warrant still out for his arrest, Voltaire couldn't get a visa for the States, so he coudn't fly up to El Paso to check out the stud ranch firsthand. But I didn't know anything about that when I went down to Madera.

I was seventeen, wore my pants skin tight and greased my hair straight back, thought I could do anything and fancied myself all of a man. I enjoyed every opportunity to prove it. Dad gave me that chance by sending me to Rancho Francaise with a suitcase full of papers.

• • •

Delta Airlines had a daily milkrun that winged through the airport in Madera every morning at nine en route to Belize, then skipped by again at eleven-thirty P.M. on its rebound to El Paso and beyond. That midnight special would be my salvation, but I wasn't thinking about that when I stepped off the plane and was walloped by the heat. I staggered into the little airport structure and met Voltaire. My red hair and fair skin threw him because, I imagine, no one had ever told him I wasn't Hispanic (but had been adopted by people who were). Anyway, he relaxed at hearing my fluid Spanish, snapped his fingers, a barefoot kid dashed over and grabbed my bag and we made our way out to his Jeep.

Jean-Paul Rouart—"Voltaire"—was maybe five-foot eight, 150 pounds, and walked with the swagger of Napoleon at Versailles. His face and arms were bronzed like the mestizo he was, his hands fiercely calloused, the index and middle finger on his right hand stained brown from the fifty or so cigarettes he huffed a day. He smelled like a dump fire, and I told him so. He flashed me a mean little grin, but kept the windows down in his Jeep as we rolled through town. It took about thirty minutes to drive out to Rancho Francaise.

The Rancho Francaise hacienda consisted of a low sprawl of cement *quartos*, darned together with mortar and huge oaken beams garlanded with bougainvillea and dahlias. The sun blistered the surrounding terrain, but it was shady and cool inside the hacienda.

With a flick of the hand, Voltaire directed his wife, Dona Barbara, to get me something to eat, then he vanished into his study with my documents. Dona Barbara was a gracious hostess, her black hair twisted up into a bun and held there with tortoise shell hairpins, her torso so surfeited with frijoles and lard and all things frita that she resembled an overripe Bartlett pear with legs. It was Dona Barbara's honor to never, if she could help it, go outside, and she was pale as a jailbird. Not so Marie, Dona Barbara's daughter. A couple years older than I, she'd just finished her first year at the University in Durango, about 100 miles south of Rancho Francaise. Marie had dreamy chocolate skin, a defiant tilt to her head and the frame of an Olympic gymnast set off by a wee red halter top she wore tight as the cellophane on a new CD. I kept shifting around the kitchen, knowing there had to be something more worthwhile than watching Marie wash that gourd, but for the life of me I couldn't tell what it was. I'm positive she realized I was staring at her, for they always know—and I wanted her to know anyway. The second I saw her my mind jumped straight into bed.

"You have an excellent capacity for sweating," she finally said.

"You should see me draw," I said.

"Will you draw me?"

"If you'll pose."

"In what?" she smiled, good health and animal spirits flashing through her eyes.

I was just working up a leading answer when Voltaire returned and we both left to take a look at Rancho Francaise.

Rancho Francaise sat in the eastern shadow of the Sierra Madres from which a river gushed and veined out across Rancho Francaise's 6,000 hectares. A colonnade of trees and herbage ran with the rivers and creeks criss-crossing Rancho Francaise, but fifty feet from the water it was all prickly pear, scrub oak and creosote. Flanking Rancho Francaise on all sides were rich agricultural tracts, made so by the water Voltaire doled out at ruinous prices to surrounding farmers, water that had made Voltaire a Gran Jéfé—a big boss man, with dominion over people's lives to a degree a foreigner could never comprehend.

Spread out over Rancho Francaise were dozens of levees, reservoirs and aqueducts that required great vigilance and even greater labor to maintain. Near each site rested a few cinder block and adobe huts, the homes of peon families whose only mission in life was to regulate water levels and watch gates and work the site as required. We spent the remains of the day going from one site to the other. Voltaire literally dove for the sledge or pickax, slaving in lockstep with his dozens of peons—pouring concrete, mixing mortar and humping 30-kilo bags of gravel on his back under a brutal sun. I figured myself equal to any of these folk, so I grabbed a pick and found that I wasn't.

• • •

Voltaire worked like a dog not simply to show all who was boss, but also to humble me, to exhaust the sass out of me, for Voltaire was too much full of Voltaire to have some teenage gringo waltz into Rancho Francaise and cast airs. I hated feeling so useless, so I humped bags and swung at that flinty soil like a fiend—and made an ass of myself. By the time we returned to the hacienda at sundown, I was already nodding.

"We'll get a full day in tomorrow," Voltaire chuckled as I straggled back to my room to collapse for an hour.

That night after dinner, Voltaire moved to the veranda and gave audience to dozens of Rancho Francaise peons—a nightly ritual. Various dogs hung close to the sides of certain peons, though they were not the peon's dogs. A peon didn't have the right to own a dog. Voltaire did not allow it. The dogs, the land, the water, the peons themselves all belonged to Voltaire, who demanded their eternal fealty. They were not even free to leave. That was bald-faced betrayal of a benefactor. Marie later told me how every couple years a peon would run off, inevitably ending up drunk and soul dead in some gutter. The Federales would first thrash him, then "fine" him for all his pockets bore, then drag him back to Voltaire, who would send him off to clear great tracts of brambles and thistles in distant quadrants of Rancho Francaise.

After coffee and sweets all around, Voltaire listened gravely to the preoccupations that governed his human community. Clearly, the dozen or so peons around him, and everyone else but Marie for that matter, lived according to Voltaire's moods, and they were forever trying to invoke the good ones. It was always "Si, mi jéfé," and "As you wish, mi jéfé." His very presence honored them, and he was rich enough to believe everything he said, responding with insufferably sluggish speech, as though each comment was a divine mandate performed at ritual speed. He was impressive in his self-command, but sitting on that veranda I knew no matter how high he built his throne, he'd still be sitting on his ass.

Later that first night, I lounged around Marie's room and watched her composing doggerel on a home computer—one of the first ones I'd ever seen. We were not alone. Voltaire insisted a chaperon be present, and the door be left open as well—to preserve the virgin's honor, I suppose, which tells how much Voltaire really knew. Nevertheless, Voltaire's orders were the law at Rancho Francaise.

Marie's computer had a graphics program, and after some tinkering I came up with some interesting geometric stuff. Marie took over and kept fiddling and punching. She was just like Voltaire in that she always had to keep occupied, whereas if I wasn't painting or reading I made an occupation of dreaming and wasting time. Nothing I could ever say or do would land us horizontal, not with the door open and a *domestica* breathing down our necks, but I tried everything I could think of to get a smile out of her. She seemed friendly enough, but was the kind you can never read for certain, and eventually I got so groggy I had to go.

"Your father's a workhorse," I said, trying to explain away my fatigue.

"He's an ass," she growled in accented English. She looked right at me when she said it. Then a smile. A crazy smile. Rancho Francaise was heating up.

The next two days passed much the same as the first, me trying desperately to keep pace with Voltaire by day, and trying even more desperately to enchant Marie by night. I had that pickax moving like a bee's wing—to little result; but I was turning a little ground with Marie, or hoped I was. The difference between a seventeen-year-old boy and a nineteen-year-old woman is an age, so I still didn't know if I was hauling ashes or sugar.

On my third and last night in Rancho Francaise a peon named Bonifacio wobbled up to the veranda, his face horribly swollen on one side. He mumbled something, and Voltaire sat him down on a stool, pried his mouth open with his hands and peered inside as though he were eyeballing a well.

"It's abscessed, Bonifacio. It's got to come out."

"Por favor, mi jéfé," Bonifacio moaned.

"Of course." Voltaire looked over to me and said, "Doug, get my tools. In the truck."

For three days my only breaks had come when I'd fetch Voltaire's shovel, his lighter, his canteen. It all went to confirm who was boss and who was lackey, and he'd done an exhausting job of it. He flipped me his keys and I wandered out to his truck.

Hell yes I was jealous of Voltaire—jealous of his menacing presence and rudeness of power, his capacity to work me into the tundra. But mostly, I resented how this sham Frenchman had maneuvered me into the same furrow as all the other three-peso guttersnipes he had under his boot heel, jumping at his every command, doing everything but dropping to my knees in brute compunction and *still* coming back with, "Si, mi jéfé," "As you wish, mi jéfé," "Como tu permission, mi jéfé." Fuck you, mi jéfé, I yelled into the night, walking out to his truck.

Digging around for the tools, realizing Voltaire was going to yank Bonifacio's tooth, I thought how peculiar it was that Voltaire would own dental instruments—and keep them with his tools. I couldn't find them, and lugged the whole toolbox to the veranda. Voltaire rummaged through the ratchets and wrenches and drew out a greasy pair of long-nosed pliers. Dona Barbara boiled them in mescal, and Voltaire was ready. Bonifacio only thought he was.

Bonifacio opened his swollen mouth and Voltaire began probing with the pliers; but with the first clutch of steel on his abscessed tooth Bonifacio shot off the stool like it was the electric chair, dropped to his knees and rocked back and forth, both hands clutching his jaw, begging Voltaire's forgiveness, swearing the tooth wasn't so bad after all, that given time the pain would surely go away and that he was going home.

"It must come out." Voltaire glanced to several peons and nodded, and the peons took Bonifacio by the arms and installed him back on the stool. "Hold him," Voltaire said grimly. The peons each took an arm or a leg. "Now open up, Bonifacio, and let's get this over with."

The tooth was set so far back in Bonifacio's mouth that Voltaire looked like he was working on his tonsils. As he started yanking and twisting the pliers, Bonifacio's legs flailed the veranda. Two men got on each arm and two more held his mouth open as Voltaire wrenched away, really earning his money now, twisting Bonifacio's head side to side.

I stared on in the dizzy stupor you find yourself in when witnessing torture firsthand—wanting to look away, yet transfixed by the ghastly draw of it all.

Suddenly, a dull pop. Voltaire removed the pliers, and gripped in the end was a gory tooth. Or rather, half of a tooth. It had snapped off flush with the gums.

"Gran puta de la madre," Voltaire grumbled, glaring at the crown of red tooth, then flicking it into the sand. "It's no good, Bonifacio. I only got half of it." Bonifacio was gone, sobbing and shaking horribly.

"Tequila," Voltaire said, "The man needs tequila." I fetched the tequila.

"You must drink, Bonifacio," Voltaire said. "To kill the pain." Voltaire put the bottle to Bonifacio's lips and it rattled against his buck teeth. Between pants and sobs perhaps a quarter of the bottle went down his throat, while the rest streamed out the sides of his mouth.

"The pain is a great pain, I know," Voltaire consoled.

Once Bonifacio had slumped down in a daze of shock and drink, Voltaire glanced over to me and said, "You're going to have to help us hold him down, Doug." We all took an arm or a leg, Voltaire again pried open Bonifacio's mouth and, pliers in hand, had at it. The clamp of steel to his jaw jolted Bonifacio back to life and it took ten hands hold him. Shrieking and thrashing horribly, I let his leg get away from me and he kicked me so hard my nose bled for half an hour.

"Give me a hand here," Voltaire yelled, dismissing me with a wave of his hand. Someone else grabbed Bonifacio's leg and I tumbled back, holding my bloody nose and feeling like a boy.

• • •

"The man needs tequila," a peon said once the job was over.

"We all do," Voltaire added, glancing over to me. That was my cue to head back to the hacienda for another bottle, the bottle I wanted to break over his head, then cut his throat with.

"You must drink, Bonifacio," Voltaire said.

"Si, Bonifacio," another put in, "to kill the pain."

"And reduce the swelling," someone else said.

Bonifacio looked like he'd just been hanged but the rope had snapped; he hurt honestly, but forced a relieved smile. He put the bottle to his lips. Again. And again. And the other men joined in because they could. The medicinal utility of tequila is peerless and uncontested, for there is no pain or sickness that the cactus juice cannot master. If one bottle does not succeed, you punish another one.

Within an hour, I'd returned to the hacienda a dozen times, for Bonifacio's pain was a great pain. But Voltaire was a poor drinker. They all were. In Mexico, drunkenness is a thing of huge ugliness, but is inevitable because to refuse is a sign of weakness, while to drink is the mark of a man. There's a saying down there: Under a bad poncho is often a good drinker.

After another hour, all the peons had staggered off into the sage, and I had to drape one of Voltaire's arms over my shoulder and half-drag him to his room and flop him onto his bed. He was dead to the world before I'd pulled his boots off.

Later that night, nothing stirred but the breeze murmuring through the Piru trees outside my room. I lay motionless on my bed, floating over the last few days, but none of the images carried me off to sleep, so I just lay there in the shadows. When I felt the warm naked torso over my hips and saw Marie's come-to-Jesus eyes, I thought I was finally dreaming. She put her finger over my lips, whispered, "*Calmete*, Doug," leaned down and kissed me.

But Voltaire. *Christo!* If he caught us, we were both crow bait. Yet just an hour before he'd had so much liquor on board that the Spanish Armada couldn't have hauled his ass from bed. Dona Barbara knocked off every night at eight, and I could hear her hurricane snoring. And here, I foolishly believed, was my chance to settle up with Voltaire and be the man I thought I was. I kissed Marie.

Marie leaned back and moved her knees forward as I slid my thumbs down along the moist crease of her hips and past the spare raven down of her sex, up over her shuddering ribs and ran my palms lightly under her flawless globes, which were not so large but perfect, with those miraculous, upswept nipples pointing straight to the heavens, where God was surely nodding in acknowledgement of some of his finest work. I ran my hands over her superb rump. No artist could ever capture its majesty. She stayed up there on top, rocking slightly and we started moving against each other, finding each other's rhythm, slow, but gaining momentum, like a runaway train. Rivulets of sweat ran down over her taut brown stomach and I licked them and suckled her, looking up into dark eyes that were ages away, and she reached down and threaded the needle for me. She put her hand behind my head and pulled me into a kiss as I probed the crease of her rump and touched the quivering ring of her asshole, which convulsed with the muscles of her sex. She reached back and bobbled my balls and we were operating in midair now, sprinting in the thin atmosphere above the edge of ourselves. She kept grinding and gasping and I tried everything to stay the course and keep the lightning inside me, thinking about swinging the pickax through my foot and pulling my own teeth with pliers as Marie swiveled on top in a magical nimbus, her mouth slackened and sucking down huge mouthfuls of air now, head bobbing with the pulse and time melted into itself.

Then, through the little triangle of space between Marie's legs I saw him, Voltaire, leaning against the threshold for balance. If his expression could have been put into words and the words solidified, they could have dammed the Rio Grande in flood. That face. I'll take it to the grave—the face of a jéfé double-crossed, taken for a chump, his honor and dignity ripped from his heart with a clawhammer, flattened with a steam-roller, minced with hot daggers, pissed, spat and shat upon, then shoved down his throat in the choking entré of his most precious "virgin," ploughing the gringo guest. Of course, she was no more a virgin than I was a Emiliano Zapata—or a man, for that matter—but this was beside the point to the psychopath leaning against the threshold.

I couldn't move. For a few interminable seconds Marie carried on unaware, up on her knees, working the very quick of my peter, her body tense as blue steel, bearing down for keeps now, realizing it was her pleasure that counted. Through the small triangular gap between our hips and her legs I could see Voltaire, actually having to peer round my very pud to regard all of his ghastly mask. We were both paralyzed, and for those few seconds, as Marie ground on for the Promise Land, I kept jockeying my head this way and that, hiding behind my member as the pickpocket cowers behind the lamppost, Voltaire jerking his head side to side, trying to see around the blockade and rivet me until Marie finally clove herself down, clutched her breasts and flung her head back with a low, climactic sigh.

And Voltaire sprang.

He was very drunk and very crazed, and he groped and swung at the air as Marie quickly wiggled off. I grabbed my pants and fled his grasp as Marie ran for her life, losing a clump of hair to the gran jéfe. He charged after me, but stumbled at the door and crashed down two cement stairs and lay in a heap at the bottom with a gash over his eye. He was still dead-drunk, but that fall was so fortunate I thought the devil must have tripped him, though I still didn't have a clue what the hell I was going to do. Voltaire started to grumble and move. I struggled into my pants, heard the jingling and yes, I still had Voltaire's car keys from fetching his toolbox. I hurtled over Voltaire and back into the house, grabbed my shirt and shoes and ran into Marie, who'd jumped into a dress and sandals.

We drove flat out to the airport.

I just made the last Delta milkrun returning to El Paso, and Marie, laughing and cursing her father because she was crazy after all, kissed me and blasted for her uncle's in El Salto.

• • •

More than a dozen years later I returned to Rancho Francaise. Maybe it was because I'd heard Marie was still single, had gotten her law degree and was working somewhere in the Yucatan for CorpoMex. I had hauled that one night around with me all those years, had hauled it through college, through a spoiled marriage and into my thirties and it still glittered in my mind. Or part of it did. I could still see Voltaire's ghastly face and wanted to change the expression on it so I wouldn't have to see it on my deathbed. I also wanted Voltaire to see me as a grown man who had thirty men under him, managing the stud ranch, which, owing to the original debacle with Voltaire and then-sagging beef prices, my father never sold. ("Hell, Doug, Voltaire don't need no stud ranch now," my dad said at the time. "He'll just hire you.") I had worked hard to get where I was and wanted once and for all to set straight those days of dragging around after Voltaire like another one of his peons. So I flew down to Madera on the spur of the moment, rented a car and drove out to Rancho Francaise.

Voltaire—who hadn't aged a day—answered the door, knocked me flat with one punch, glared at me for a long moment, then pulled me to my feet and led me over to the veranda. I deserved that punch, told Voltaire so, and to my surprise, the affair was put behind us with a wave of his hand. But it didn't take me long to get back to Marie.

"Married," said Voltaire, with an edge in his voice. She'd married some fancy attorney working out of the governor's office. I told Voltaire that was a damn shame, but that Marie deserved the best she could get. I also made a stab at formally apologizing about that night, fumbled out a few sentences and Voltaire held up his hand again and said, "I'll be married thirty-three years, this June. Marie was thirty-three on April 14th." He chuckled. "I didn't get married by choice, but at the end of my father-in-law's shotgun, just like you would have if you'd stuck around."

"I wish I had," I said.

Voltaire said that, judging by his son-in-law's Italian shoes, linen shirts and genuine cologne ("The bastard must bathe in the stuff.") that he wished I'd stuck around as well. Then he declared that we both needed drinks. He didn't have any liquor in the house, but had a bottle under the seat in his truck. He flipped me his keys.

A Real Man

Feb. 12, 1920

Editor of the Daily News:

So the girls say there's "no such animal" as a "real man" eh? I'll say there's no such thing as a "real woman." When a girl calls you "honey" or "cupcake" don't believe her. A criminal calls the judge "Your Honor."

—M.S.

Turkish Bath
by Mark Twain

For years and years and years I have dreamed of the wonders of the Turkish Bath; for years and years I have promised myself that I would yet enjoy one. Many and many a time, in fancy, I have lain in the marble bath, and breathed the slumberous fragrance of Eastern spices that filled the air; then passed through a weird and complicated system of pulling and hauling, and drenching and scrubbing, by a gang of naked savages who loomed vast and vaguely through the steaming mists, like demons; then rested for a while on a divan fit for a king; then passed through another complex ordeal, and one more fearful than the first; and, finally, swathed in soft fabrics, been conveyed to a princely saloon and laid on a bed of eider down, where eunuchs, gorgeous of costume, fanned me while I drowsed and dreamed, or contentedly gazed at the rich hangings of the apartment, the soft carpets, the sumptuous furniture, the pictures, and drank delicious coffee, smoked the soothing narghili, and dropped, at the last, into tranquil repose, lulled by the sensuous odors from unseen censers, by the gentle influence of narghili's Persian tobacco, and by the music of fountains that counterfeited the pattering of summer rain.

That was the picture, just as I got it from incendiary books of travel. It was a poor, miserable imposture. The reality is no more like it than the Five Points are like the Garden of Eden. They received me in a great court, paved with marble slabs; around it were broad galleries, one above another, carpeted with seedy matting, railed with unpainted balustrades, and furnished with huge rickety chairs, cushioned with rusty old mattresses indented with impressions left by the forms of nine successive generations of men who had reposed upon them. The place was vast, naked, dreary; its court a barn, its galleries stalls for human horses. The cadaverous, half nude varlets that served in the establishment had nothing of poetry in their appearance, nothing of romance, nothing of Oriental splendor. They shed no entrancing odors—just the contrary. Their hungry eyes and their lank forms continually suggested one glaring, unsentimental fact—they wanted what they term in California "a square meal."

I went into one of the racks and undressed. An unclean starveling wrapped a gaudy tablecloth about his loins, and hung a white rag over my shoulders. If I had a tub then, it would have come natural to me to take in washing. I was then conducted down stairs into the wet, slippery court, and the first things that attracted my attention were my heels. My fall excited no comment. They expected it, no doubt. It belonged in the list of softening, sensuous influences peculiar to this home of Eastern luxury. It was softening enough, certainly, but its application was not happy. They now gave me a pair of wooden clogs—benches in miniature, with leather straps over them to confine my feet (which they would have done, only I do not wear No. 13s.) These things dangled uncomfortably by the straps when I lifted up my feet, and came down in awkward and unexpected places when I put them on the floor again, and sometimes turned sideways and wrenched my ankles out of joint. However, it was all Oriental luxury and I did what I could to enjoy it.

They put me in another part of the barn and laid me on a stuffy sort of pallet, which was not made of cloth of gold, or Persian shawls, but was merely the unpretending sort of thing I have seen in the negro quarters of Arkansas. There was nothing whatever in this dim marble prison but five more of these biers. It was a very solemn place. I expected that the spiced odors of Araby were going to steal over my senses now, but they did not. A copper-colored skeleton, with a rag around him, brought me a glass decanter of water, with a lighted tobacco pipe on top of it, and a pliant stem a yard long, with a brass mouth-piece to it.

It was the famous "narghili" of the East—the thing the Grand Turk smokes in pictures. This began to look like luxury. I took one blast at it, and it was sufficient; the smoke went in a great volume down into my stomach, my lungs, into the uttermost parts of my frame. I exploded one mighty cough, and it was as if Vesuvius had let go. For the next five minutes I smoked at every pore, like a frame house that is on fire on the inside. Not any more narghili for me. The smoke had a vile taste, and the taste of a thousand infidel tongues that remained on that brass mouthpiece was viler still. I was getting discouraged. Whenever, hereafter, I see the cross-legged Grand Turk smoking his narghili, in pretended bliss, on the outside of a paper of Connecticut tobacco, I shall know him for the shameless humbug he is.

The prison was filled with hot air. When I had got warmed up sufficiently to prepare me for a still warmer temperature, they took me where it was—into a marble room, wet, slippery and steamy, and laid me out on a raised platform in the center. It was very warm. Presently my man sat me down by a tank of hot water, drenched me well, gloved his hand with a coarse mitten, and began to polish me all over with it. I began to smell disagreeably. The more he polished the worst I smelt. It was alarming. I said to him:

"I perceive that I am pretty far gone. It is plain that I ought to be buried without any unnecessary delay. Perhaps you had better go after my friends at once, because the weather is warm, and I cannot 'keep' for long."

He went on scrubbing, and paid no attention. I soon saw that he was reducing my size. He bore hard on his mitten, and from under it rolled little cylinders, like macaroni. It could not be dirt, for it was too white. He pared me down in this way for a long time. Finally I said:

"It is a tedious process. It will take hours to trim me to the size you want me; I will wait; go and borrow a jack-plane."

He paid no attention at all.

After awhile he brought a basin, some soap, and something that resembled the tail of a horse. He made up a prodigious quantity of soap-suds, deluged me with them from head to foot, without warning me to shut my eyes, and then swabbed me viciously with the horse-tail. Then he left me there, a snowy statue of lather, and went away. When I got tired of waiting I went and hunted him up. He was propped against the wall, in another room, asleep. I woke him. He was not disconcerted. He took me back and flooded me with hot water, then turbaned my head, swathed me with dry tablecloths, and conducted me to a latticed chicken-coop in one of the galleries, and pointed to one of those Arkansas beds. I mounted it, and vaguely expected the odors of Araby again. They did not come.

The blank, unornamented coop had nothing about it of that oriental voluptuousness one reads of so much. It was more suggestive of the county hospital than anything else. The skinny servitor brought a narghili, and I got him to take it out again without wasting any time about it. Then he brought the world-renowned Turkish coffee that poets have sung so rapturously for many generations, and I seized upon it the last hope that was left of my old dreams of Eastern luxury. It was another fraud. Of all the unchristian beverages that ever passed my lips, Turkish coffee is the worst. The cup is small, it is smeared with grounds; the coffee is black, thick, unsavory of smell, and execrable in taste. The bottom of the cup has a muddy sediment in it half an inch deep. This goes down your throat, and portions of it lodge by the way, and produce a tickling aggravation that keeps you barking and coughing for an hour.

Here endeth my experience of the celebrated Turkish bath, and here also endeth my dream of the bliss the mortal revels in who passes through it. It is a magnificent swindle. The man who enjoys it is qualified to enjoy any thing that is repulsive to sight or sense, and he that can invest it with a charm of poetry is able to do the same with any thing else in the world that is tedious, and wretched, and dismal, and nasty.

—from *Innocents Abroad*

What To Do With All Those "Free" Soaps When Traveling
by Shelley Berman

According to the Sunday (London) Times, in which this piece first appeared, the following is actual correspondence between a guest in a London hotel and the hotel staff.

Dear Maid,

Please do not leave any more of those little bars of soap in my bathroom since I have brought my own bath-sized Dial. Please remove the six unopened little bars from the shelf under the medicine chest and another three in the shower soap dish. They are in my way.

—*Thank you,*
S. Berman

Dear Room 635,

I am not your regular maid. She will be back tomorrow, Thursday, from her day off. I took the 3 hotel soaps out of the shower dish as you requested. The 6 bars on your shelf I took out of your way and put them on top of your Kleenex dispenser in case you should change your mind. This leaves only the 3 bars I left today which my instructions from the management is to leave 3 soaps daily.

I hope this is satisfactory.

—*Kathy, Relief Maid*

Dear Maid — I hope you are my regular maid.

Apparently Kathy did not tell you about my note to her concerning the little bars of soap. When I got back to my room this evening I found you had added 3 little Camays to the shelf under the medicine cabinet.

I am going to be here in the hotel for two weeks and have brought my own bath-size Dial so I won't need those 6 little Camays which are on the shelf. They are in my way when shaving, brushing my teeth, etc. Please remove them.

—*S. Berman*

Dear Mr. Berman,

My day off was last Wed. so the relief maid left 3 hotel soaps which we're instructed by the management. I took the 6 soaps which were in your way on the shelf and put them in the soap dish where your Dial was. I put the Dial in the medicine cabinet for your convenience. I didn't remove the 3 complimentary soaps which are always placed inside the medicine cabinet for all new check-ins and which you did not object to when you checked in last Monday. Please let me know if I can be of further assistance.

—Your regular maid, Dotty

Dear Mr. Berman,

The assistant manager, Mr. Kensedder, informed me this A.M. that you called him last evening and said you were unhappy with your maid service. I have assigned a new girl to your room. I hope you will accept my apologies for any past inconvenience. If you have future complaints please contact me so I can give it my personal attention. Call extension 1108 between 8 A.M. and 5 P.M.

Thank you,

—Elaine Carmen, Housekeeper

Dear Mrs. Carmen,

It is impossible to contact you by phone since I leave the hotel for business at 7:45 A.M. and don't get back before 5:30 or 6 P.M. That's the reason I called Mr. Kensedder last night. You were already off duty. I only asked Mr. Kensedder if he could do anything about those little bars of soap. The new maid you assigned me must have thought I was a new check-in today, since she left another 3 bars of hotel soap in my medicine cabinet along with her regular delivery of 3 bars on the bathroom shelf. In just 5 days here I have accumulated 24 little bars of soap. Why are you doing this to me?

—S. Berman

Dear Mr. Berman,

Your maid, Kathy, has been instructed to stop delivering soap to your room and remove the extra soaps. If I can be of further assistance, please call extension 1108 between 8 A.M. and 5 P.M.

Thank you,

—Elaine Carmen, Housekeeper

What To Do With All Those "Free" Soaps When Traveling

Dear Mr. Kensedder,

My bath-size Dial is missing. Every bar of soap was taken from my room including my own bath-size Dial. I came in late last night and had to call the bellhop to bring me 4 little Cashmere Bouquets.

—*S. Berman*

Dear Mr. Berman,

I have informed our housekeeper, Elaine Carmen, of your soap problem. I cannot understand why there was no soap in your room since our maids are instructed to leave 3 bars of soap each time they service a room. The situation will be rectified immediately. Please accept my apologies for the inconvenience.

—*Martin L. Kensedder, Assistant Manager*

Dear Mrs. Carmen,

Who the hell left 54 little bars of Camay in my room? I came in last night and found 54 little bars of soap. I don't want 54 little bars of Camay. I want my one damn bar of bath-size Dial. Do you realize that I have 54 bars of soap in here. All I want is my bath-size Dial. Please give me back my bath-size Dial.

—*S. Berman*

Dear Mr. Berman,

You complained of too much soap in your room so I had them removed. Then you complained to Mr. Kensedder that all your soap was missing so I personally returned them. The 24 Camays which had been taken and the 3 Camays which you are supposed to receive daily (sic). I don't know anything about the 4 Cashmere Bouquets. Obviously, your maid, Kathy, did not know I had returned your soaps, so she also brought 24 Camays plus the 3 daily Camays. I don't know where you got the idea this hotel issues bath-size Dial. I was able to locate some bath-size Ivory which I left in your room.

—*Elaine Carmen, Housekeeper*

Dear Mrs. Carmen,

Just a note to bring you up-to-date on my latest soap inventory. As of today I possess:

- On the shelf under the medicine cabinet - 18 Camay in 4 stacks of 4 and 1 stack of 2.
- On Kleenex dispenser - 11 Camay in 2 stacks of 4 and 1 stack of 3.

• On bedroom dresser - 1 stack of 3 Cashmere Bouquet, 1 stack of 4 hotel-size Ivory, and 8 Camay in 2 stacks of 4.
• Inside medicine cabinet - 14 Camay in 3 stacks of 4 and 1 stack of 2.
• In shower soap dish - 6 Camay, very moist.
• On northeast corner of tub - 1 Cashmere Bouquet, slightly used.
• On northwest corner of tub - 6 Camays in 2 stacks of 3.

Please ask Kathy when she services my room to make sure the stacks are neatly piled and dusted. Also, please advise her that stacks of more than 4 have a tendency to tip. May I suggest that my bedroom window sill is not in use and will make an excellent spot for future soap deliveries. One more item, I have purchased another bar of bath-sized Dial which I am keeping in the hotel vault in order to avoid further misunderstandings.

—*S. Berman*